THE FARMERS HOTEL

John O'Hara

THE
FARMERS HOTEL

BARRIE & JENKINS
COMMUNICA - EUROPA

© 1953 by John O'Hara

First published in 1953 by
The Cresset Press Ltd., 11 Fitzroy Square, London W1
Reprinted 1978 by Barrie and Jenkins
24 Highbury Crescent
London N5 1RX

ISBN 0 248 65067 X

Printed in Great Britain by litho at The Anchor Press Ltd
and bound by Wm Brendon & Son Ltd
both of Tiptree, Essex

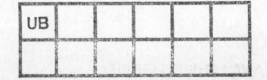

Part One

ROCKBOTTOM, PA., a village of 352 souls, is in lower Macungie County about equidistant from Allentown and Bethlehem. Dieglersville, six miles to the east and with a population of 2,248, is the nearest town of any size. The other villages around Rockbottom are, clockwise, Flour Mill, Heffelfinger, Wheelwright, Sanctuary, and Asa. They are all under the 1,000 population mark and, in fact, Asa is carried on census rolls at a nominal 40, representing neither gain nor loss since 1920.

Dieglersville, although by-passed by the six-lane, modernized version of the Old Turnpike, is an important bus-stop and has no fewer than eight tourist camps or motel establishments. It also has two banks, four Protestant churches, a knitting mill, two fire companies, the Lutheran Orphans' Asylum, a high school with an indoor swimming pool, a three-story American Legion home, and a Clinic, which is owned and operated by four physicians and a dentist. Dieglersville in addition is the site of the Diegler Caves, which are visited annually by upwards of 50,000 persons, according to figures made available by the Junior Chamber of Commerce.

Rockbottom has no bank, no mill of any kind, and only one church, the Lutheran. Rockbottom boys and girls go to Dieglersville High, Rockbottom veterans belong to the Dieglersville Legion post, if there are any interesting caves underneath Rockbottom, they have not been discovered. If a Rockbottom citizen is taken with acute appendicitis he has to be rushed to the Moyer Clinic in Dieglersville. The one thing that distinguishes Rockbottom from Flour Mill, Heffelfinger, Wheelwright, Sanctuary, Asa, and Dieglersville too, is the Farmers Hotel. Rockbottom still has a farmers' hotel, with Ira Studebaker to run it.

This little story of Ira Studebaker and his Farmers Hotel opens in late November a year ago, at a moment when one phase of Ira Studebaker's work was just ending and another phase just about to begin.

It was getting dark outside. Ira went around turning on the electricity in the lobby and the dining-room and the bar, turning on every lamp, putting his fingers to the toggle switch and looking up at the lamp in anticipation of the light that was to come, but a little apprehensive of a power or bulb failure. Each time the light came he nodded slightly and half smiled.

When all the lights were on he went behind the bar, tried the beer taps, inspected the bottled goods, and held a shell glass up to the light. He lifted the lids of the brass cuspidors to make sure they contained water, and he ran his fingers along the mahogany bar and the back-bar, but he did not look at his fingers; he knew there could be no dust so soon, for he had attended to the dusting himself within the hour—as indeed he had checked up on the beer pump and the whisky supply and everything else, personally and not many minutes before.

The coal fire was burning efficiently in the bar-room stove and in the stove in the adjoining lobby; the chairs were placed casually and invitingly in both rooms, and the registry lay open on the curved desk. Ira Studebaker dipped pen in ink and was about to write something on the registry, but on one of his earlier rounds he had written the date, and there did not seem to be anything else to write so he stuck the pen

11

back in the potato. He rubbed his hands down his vest four or five times, a gesture that he often made when wondering what to do next. Suddenly he reached out and tapped the bell that was beside the registry. The ringing from the third tap had not died down when a man in a white jacket entered the lobby from the dining-room. He was a tall, thin Negro, whose features could have been the model for a portrait of an officer in the Confederate cavalry. He limped slightly —interestingly and not in the seriously handi-capped sense. He carried a feather duster.

"Yes, sir," he said.

"Oh, I didn't mean to bother you, Charles," said Ira Studebaker.

"That's all right. I wasn't doing anything," said Charles, whose full name was Charles Moultrie Mannering. "Just sitting back there in the kitchen. This duster, it ain't even for show. Just didn't think to put it back in the closet."

"Well, everything seems all right to me. All in readiness," said Ira Studebaker.

"Appears to be," said Charles.

"The only thing I didn't test was the bell," said Ira Studebaker.

"It came loud and clear all the way back to the

kitchen. That is, if it was three times you rung it. Three rings was what I heard."

"That's how many times I rang," said Ira. "But not too loud, I hope. I wouldn't want it to be too loud."

"I wouldn't let that worry you if I was you. I always like to hear the bell ringing in a hotel. You know: 'Bing! Front, boy.' I always like that."

"Yes, you're right. I never thought of that before, but it's a fact," said Ira.

"Three rings, maybe that ain't so good. But one ring, I like the sound of it," said Charles. "Unless you mean three for some kind of a signal."

"We'll have to arrange a set of signals. One for one thing, and two for something else," said Ira. "What would two stand for?"

"Well, one stands for 'Front, boy'. Two—I don't know what two should stand for. We ought to wait and see if we're gonna need a two."

"Yes, exactly," said Ira. "Well, I guess we're open for business. *Farmers Hotel, Rockbottom, Pa., is open for business!* Let's fling open the doors and welcome the public."

"You want me to fling open the doors? You taken a look at the weather? I'll fling 'em open,

13

if that's what you want, Mr. Studebaker, but I think we ought to close them promptly."

"Well, I'll be damned," said Ira. "Look at that snow. When did that snow start?"

"Shortly after two o'clock this afternoon, it started lightly."

"Well, I'll be," said Ira. "I've been so busy around here I never gave a thought to how it was outside. Never even looked out the window, all afternoon."

"I said to myself around three o'clock, I said if this keeps up we'll start out busy. The transient trade. We ought to do a big supper business. I said so to Mrs. Fenstermacher."

"We're pretty far from any main road, Charles," said Ira Studebaker.

"I know, that's what you said all along. But when you got a heavy fall of snow, like this one here, people get lost from not reading signs. Some fellow gets a flat tyre and he don't want to fix it himself. He'd rather walk a mile or two and get somebody to fix it *for* him. And if he sees a nice cheerful hotel he's gonna come in and ask us is that garage the only one in Rockbottom, and where can he get in touch with the man that owns it. Takes off his coat and has a toddy. Nice warm stove.

14

Two or three more toddies. Do we serve supper?
Do we have rooms? Why should he walk all the
way back to that car in all this snow? Spend the
night here in this nice warm hotel, with all these
surroundings. Where's the telephone? Calls up. 'Ed,
my car broke down in a place called Rockbottom.
Snowing like hell here, so I'm gonna spend the night
at the Farmers Hotel. See you in the morning.' "

"You think it'll work out that way, Charles?"
said Ira.

"If there's a man in that predicament. I ain't
saying that's the only way, but I guarantee you,
we'll have rooms occupied tonight. I bet we do
a good supper business. That's what I told Mrs.
Fenstermacher."

"Is she prepared for it? Yes, of course she is,"
said Ira.

"Oh, prepared, all right. But sceptical. She said
that's the way it'd of been when there was horses
and carriages. But automobile people, they want
to hurry to one of them modern hotels in Allentown or Bethlehem. But I said, yes, but maybe
they'll hurry themselves into a ditch, and any
port in a storm. So she said to me, 'Charles, you
been right about so many things, maybe you'll
be right about this.' "

15

"I hope so. Not that I want to get business out of people's misfortune."

"I look at it the other way," said Charles. "What a lucky thing for those people we're *in* business. A nice clean warm hotel, comfortable. Honest people running it. In the olden days, you know, the traveller that stopped at the first inn he come across, he run a pretty good chance of getting his throat cut and nothing more ever heard of him. That was a common practice in merrie England. If it was me, I'd be mighty pleased to have a little mishap and discover a place like this."

"Thank you, Charles," said Ira.

"Sure," said Charles.

"You reminded me of something," said Ira. He went to the front door and removed the large brass key. "You speaking of England reminded me of this. I think it was England. Here, your arm is better than mine." He handed the key to Charles. "Throw it as far as you can."

"Outside?" said Charles.

"Right. I remember reading about some hotel, or maybe it was a lot of hotels, a custom. Where they threw the key away the day they opened the hotel."

"I remember it," said Charles. The two men went out on the front porch. "Which direction'll I throw it?"

"Suit yourself," said Ira.

"Let's see now," said Charles. "How about if I throw it over Doctor Graeff's house roof? That's a pretty good throw."

"Better than I could do," said Ira.

"Here goes," said Charles. He wound up, and hurled the key. Neither man saw the key after it left Charles' hand.

" Gone," said Ira.

" Gone all right," said Charles.

"Let's get inside, that's a thin jacket you're wearing," said Ira. They went inside and kept walking until they were in the bar-room.

"Mr. Studebaker, you know what would please me greatly?"

"What's that, Charles?"

"Well, now, you know I've been living semi-retired, so that means I must have a little money put away."

"Yes, I know that," said Ira.

" This here dollar bill, it didn't have to come from you, did it? A matter of fact, it *didn't* come from you. It was money I had before I come here.

17

I got your both cheques in my wallet. Therefore, this ain't money you paid me."

"Uh-huh."

"Right. Well, I tell you what I'd like to do. I'd like to buy the first drink under the new management. I'll buy you a drink and me a drink with this little dollar bill and you can have it framed and hung up there over the cash register."

"Say, I like that very much," said Ira. "Do you want to ring it up?"

"No, I want *you* to ring it up. I'll sign my name on it and what's the date, and you can have it framed. Also, you serve the drinks, I'm just a customer."

"Very good idea," said Ira. He moved to the duckboards behind the bar and as professionally as possible said: "What'll it be?"

"I'll take a bourbon and a water chaser. Have something on me."

"The house takes a—I guess a bourbon." Ira poured the drinks and the two men raised their glasses in mutual toast. Charles laid the dollar bill on the bar and Ira picked it up. "One dollar, right," said Ira. He rang it up on the cash register and touched the drawer with the money, but did not leave it there. Instead he held it up for Charles to see, and then tucked the bill in his vest pocket.

"Well, I guess I better start swinging the old snow shovel," said Charles.

"You got a pair of arctics?" said Ira.

"Oh, yes. I come fully prepared. I know this Pennsylvania weather." He left, and Ira came around and sat at a bar-room table and lit a cigar.

He remained there alone for half an hour. A couple of times his cigar went out and he got up and relit it at the miniature gas lamp on the lobby desk. Once or twice he stood at the double doors and peered out, but there was not much to see. The path that Charles had cleared soon had its own depth of snow. There was a single track that some automobile had made and that had been taken by two or three other cars. A path had been broken on the sidewalk across the street in front of the Lutheran church, the Klinger home, the Zumbach home, the Lloyd Fenstermacher home, and Dr. Graeff's home-and-office, which was as far as Ira Studebaker could see in that direction. Catercornered, at Kemp's garage, Ira could see only a single naked mazda lamp in Dewey Kemp's office, and the snow around the garage had not been broken in recent hours,

19

which meant that Dewey had gone home very early or he might have gone to Allentown for some auto parts. Dewey lived at the other end of town and some days did not open the garage at all except to sell gasoline to a regular customer. (He was rumoured to be working on an invention.) A vehicle of wider tread than a passenger car had passed along Wheelwright Road (which cut across Main Street to form the Farmers Hotel corner), but that too must have been hours ago.

"Oh, there'll be somebody along," said Ira to himself.

As if in reply to his thought there was a stomping on the front porch, followed by a fluttering of the American flag on the bar as someone opened the lobby door. A man's voice called out: "Hello, Ira? Anybody here?" Ira got up to greet the newcomer.

" Yes, I'm here. Hello, Henry. Come in."

The visitor, J. Henry Graeff, M.D., was wearing an old style greatcoat that must have cost a hundred and fifty dollars new. "I think I got something belongs to you," he said. "Very mystifying. Is this yours?" He held out the brass doorkey.

"Yep," said Ira. He smiled.

"Well, I wish you could explain something to me."

20

" Will if I can, Henry. Take off your coat and sit down. Have a little something to take the chill off."

" Well, I'll take off my coat a minute, but nothing to drink till after office hours. If you're going to be open after eight o'clock I'll take you up on the offer."

The doctor sat down at a table with Ira. "I was in my back office—*you* know. Bringing my books up to date. I have a young fellow comes down from Allentown once a week and does the real book-keeping, but I'm supposed to keep track of visits and office calls. Only I put it off sometimes and then I have to sit down and try to remember who I saw the last two-three days. Not that I have that many patients, but if you let it go three-four days you forget to put down who you saw Tuesday and who you saw Wednesday. When Sadie was alive I didn't have to remember. She always knew. But that's a long time ago, and I still haven't worked out a system—or followed it. I worked it out, but I don't follow it.

"Well, I was sitting there and trying to straighten out who I saw when and all of a sudden *Clang!* Something hit my car parked outside the back office. I couldn't imagine what it was but

21

I didn't like the sound of it. I only have the one car and I wouldn't want anything to happen to it, especially on a night like this. So I went out and took a look around and I happened to notice there was a hole in the snow on the hood, then down the side of the hood was this line and in the snow down as far as where the fender joins the chassis. And there, lying there, was this key. 'Now how did that get there?' I said to myself. I studied it for a minute and asked myself where a key like that'd come from. Nowadays you don't often see a key like that.

" So it's your key. I figured that out. But what I wish you'd tell me is, do you know how it got there?"

" Yes, Henry, I do," said Ira, and gave a report of the key-throwing ceremony.

"I see," said Dr. Graeff. "Well, a lot of people thought you were crazy when you took over this place. And now I know it. What else are you thinking of throwing away?"

"Nothing. Nothing at all."

"Just money and keys, that's all, eh, Ira?"

"Oh, I might throw something else away if the spirit moved me. I don't make any promises, Henry."

22

"You don't think I better have you locked up for your own good? I know of a place where they'd treat you with kindness, feed you well. It's for harmless people like you, Ira. Men about your age. They don't take violent cases. I could get a court order, you know, and there wouldn't be any more to it."

"Well, I don't know, Henry. There's only one thing wrong with that idea."

"And what's that?"

"Well, if you went into court to get a court order to put me in the crazy-house, aren't you afraid the judge would take a good look at you and tell them to lead *you* away? All I'm doing here is trying to have a little fun running a country hotel. But if a real smart judge—or a real dumb one, for that matter—if he took a good look at you, and heard you were not only running loose, but treating sick people . . . I don't know, Henry. I'd stay out of court if I were you."

"Well, suit yourself. I made the offer in a kindly spirit, but if you're considering throwing other things, be careful you don't hit Elsie Zumbach's property. You know Elsie doesn't only think you're harmless. She thinks you want to

23

open up a whore-house. That's what she thinks this place is going to turn out to be. Of course maybe she's right. It's too early to tell."

"If that's what it's going to be I bet I know who'd be the first customer," said Ira.

"I'll be back after office hours," said Dr. Graeff. He put on his greatcoat. "Here, give me back that key. If you want to get rid of it I'll drop it in Schaeffer's Dam."

"Okay, thanks," said Ira. " Say, Henry, don't say anything to Charles about this, my coloured fellow."

"Oh, I wouldn't say anything to Charles. I'm counting on Charles to shovel my snow for me tomorrow. I have to stay on his good side."

"Me too," said Ira. "See you after eight." He followed the doctor to the front door. They saw a pair of automobile lights moving slowly toward the hotel corner.

"You'd think only a doctor'd be out in this weather, and that isn't any doctor," said Graeff. The car, a station wagon, came to a halt in front of the hotel. " See you later," said Dr. Graeff.

There were two persons in the station wagon; a woman, and the driver, a man. The man got out and mounted the porch steps and addressed Ira Studebaker. "Good evening. Have you got a telephone, a pay station?"

"Sure have," said Ira. "Come right in. Does your wife want to come in and get warm?"

"Thanks, I'll see," said the man. He returned to the car, spoke to the woman—a little longer than was necessary for the simple question—and then she got out and the three went inside.

"Howdy do," said Ira to the woman.

"How do you do," said the woman.

In the light of the lobby Ira noticed for the first time that the man and the woman were wearing riding boots and breeches under their polo coats. "The phone booth, right over there in the corner there, but don't put your money in till the operator tells you. She'll say 'Number, please,' and you give the number you want and she'll tell you how much. It's different than city phones. You need any silver?"

"Will you give me a dollar in silver, please?" said the man.

"To Philadelphia is thirty-five cents," said Ira, making change from his own pocket.

"What makes you think I'm calling Philadelphia?" said the man.

25

"Well, just a guess. You look more like Philadelphia people."

"But we're not," said the man. He proceeded to the booth, closing the door behind him.

The woman warmed herself at the lobby stove, then spoke to Ira, whom she had been ignoring: "Have you any brandy?"

"Yes, ma'am, several kinds. We have——"

"Any good brandy. A pony. Two. I think the gentleman will have one too."

"The imported," said Ira.

"Yes, please," said the woman. "And where is the ladies' room?"

"Up those stairs and the first landing," said Ira.

Ira poured the brandies and put them on a tray and brought them to the lobby. The man finished his call before the woman completed her ablutions. Ira held out the tray.

"What's this? On the house?" said the man. For the first time for either of the couple, he smiled.

"Well, why not? I just opened today," said Ira.

"I was only kidding," the man said. "Actually I'd rather have a Scotch and water, if you don't mind. The brandy won't be wasted. The lady'll drink two."

26

"Any particular brand Scotch you have a preference for?"

"Oh—Ballantine's?"

"We have it," said Ira. "And water, not soda."

"Not soda," said the man. "We might as well have it in the bar, don't you think?"

"Your pleasure," said Ira. "Wherever you say."

Ira put the brandies on the bar. "I think I'll sneak one straight," said the man. "Just between you and me."

"That's right," said Ira. He filled a shot glass and the man quickly emptied it.

"You just opened today? But this is a real old-timer, isn't it? I like this kind of a place, the hell with that modern junk."

"I feel the same way, that's why I bought this place. Yes, I just opened today. In a way, you and your wife are our first customers."

"I saw another fellow leaving," said the man.

"Yes, but he didn't buy anything. He's a friend lives across the street, a doctor. No, the funny thing, our first customer was our coloured fellow." He told the Charles Mannering anecdote.

"Sounds like a very useful citizen, a man like that, place like this," said the man. He took off

27

his polo coat and laid it on a chair, just before the woman entered.

"Any luck?" she said.

"Out," said the man. "Expected back in a half to three-quarters of an hour."

"Who did you talk to, the butler?" she asked.

"Yes."

"Oh, for Christ's sake," she said, picking up a brandy and staring at it.

"Now, what else could I do?"

"I don't suppose anything," she said. She drank half the brandy, set the glass down, then drank the second half. " Are you planning to wait here for three-quarters of an hour? If so, I'd like a sandwich." She laid her coat on the chair beside the man's. She addressed Ira: "Your customers'll think you're having a costume party."

"Well, we were here first, weren't we?" said the man to Ira. To the woman he said: "We're the first customers. This gentleman just opened the place."

"Oh, come off it," said the woman.

"Tell her about it while I go to the men's room," said the man.

The brandy and the story, it seemed to Ira, were thawing her out, so that by the time the man

returned she was asking appropriate questions
with a genuine interest.

"Charming," she kept saying. "Charming."
But with the man's return and the end of the
story she resumed her earlier aloof manner.

"If you folks had time for the dinner, I can
recommend it. If you care for Pennsylvania Dutch
cooking. Real Pennsylvania Dutch. Mrs. Fenstermacher's famous all around here. Without her I
wouldn't of opened."

"I've always heard about it," said the woman.

"Mrs. Fenstermacher?" said Ira.

"No, but Pennsylvania Dutch cooking. Lived
in Pennsylvania all my life, but I'm sure——"

"Unfortunately I think we'll only have time
for a sandwich," said the man, cutting in and
talking over her. "Let's do this again? Sweetie, a
brandy, or something else?"

"A Side Car," said the woman.

"It's brandy, isn't it?" she said.

"Well, all right," said the man.

"I'll get Charles for that. I'm no good at fancy
drinks. I've *had* all the cocktails, but mixing them
is different," said Ira.

"But isn't he busy?" said the man. " Sweetie,
have another brandy."

"But I don't want another brandy, and besides I'd like to see Charles. Wouldn't *you?*"

"You don't have to worry about Charles being busy. He doesn't like it when he *isn't* busy," said Ira. " I'll ring for him." He did so, ringing once, pausing, then ringing once again. Charles appeared promptly, "Charles, this lady wants a Side Car cocktail."

"Yes, sir, yes, ma'am," said Charles. "You, sir?"

"Scotch and plain water," said the man.

"What kind of a sandwich would the lady like? Give you a nice steak sandwich with French fries. Or a roast beef, with mashed potatoes and gravy," said Ira.

"I think I'd like a steak sandwich, no potatoes. The steak quite rare and cut thin. And a cup of coffee," she said.

"I'll go for that," said the man. "But *with* the French fries. And I might have a glass of beer. I notice you have draught beer. Sweetie, some draught beer?"

"No thanks," she said.

Ira left to place the order, while Charles prepared the drinks. He did not speak until the man and woman took their first sips. "Not a very good day for hunting," he said.

"Do you know about hunting?" said the woman.

"A fair amount, a fair amount," said Charles. "I had one of my employers years ago, he had a private pack. My understanding, he gave it up in '29, due to circumstances. I was always raised around horses till I went in the Army in May '17."

"Were you in the cavalry?" the man asked.

"No, sir, I wasn't. I had a kind of a strange career in the Army," said Charles. He studied them. "I went overseas as a trombone player. I played trombone with Lieutenant Jim Europe's band, the 369th Infantry Band. I got a Purple Heart, I got a dishonourable discharge, but I can vote or get a passport just the same as anybody."

"That *is* quite a career," said the man.

"All my life I've had quite a career. You like to know how I can vote and all, even with the dishonourable?"

"By all means," said the man.

"Well, with Lieutenant Jim Europe I was stationed in Paris. The summer of '18 I happened to get a parcel of socks and chocolate, steel shaving mirror was inside, deck of playing cards. That parcel was from a lady that I once worked

31

for her husband. A note enclosed said if I ever ran into their son I was to write and tell them all about it. Well, of course I knew the son very well as a boy, and he I knew was in the Fifth Marines, so I just happened to get a furlough from the band and through a staff officer I knew, a major, I asked this major if I could be his chauffeur, because I knew this major used a general's Cadillac when he went up front, up behind the front lines on liaison. He was doing liaison with the French. That's how it happened, how I got my Purple Heart. The medal came later, much later, ten years later, but the wound I got on the 13th day of September 1918 at St. Mihiel, sitting in the driver's seat of a Cadillac automobile. I got it in the leg and like to bled to death, but at that I was better off than my major. He got his whole head decapitated by the same shrapnel hit me. I never did get to see the young man I went looking for. Never seen him to this day. I always meant to write to his mother, but by the time I got through my own troubles the war was over and everybody was back home, everybody that was gonna get there."

"Quite a story," said the man.

"They'll never get to tell all the stories happened

in *that* war. That was some war. The Second
was bigger and more global, but the First was
more like an old-fashioned *war*. An officer could
be sitting having an apéritif at a sidewalk café,
late in the afternoon. Mud on his boots. Why
didn't he get the mud taken off his boots?
Because he was going right back to his air-
drome in fifteen minutes and they'd only get all
muddy again. I saw that happen. That was a
flying officer, of course."

"What about the dishonourable discharge?"
the woman asked.

"That. Well. I went back to Lieutenant Jim
Europe's band after I was fixed up, and I guess
I thought I was John J. Pershing himself. Not
making excuses for myself, but by the time I
got back a lot of the boys got pretty uppity,
so I got just as uppity as any of them and I
decided it was time for me to light out. The war
was over and I wanted to come home and see my
family. So I just went down to Brest and bor-
rowed a pack and came home with a pioneer
outfit. I was all the way to New York Harbour
before they caught up with me, one advantage
of being a Negro in the midst of two thousand
other Negroes. Then there was a lot of red tape,

33

court martial and all that, and depriving me of my citizenship. But a former employer of mine took an interest in my case and he got me a Presidential pardon, signed Woodrow Wilson. I never even set foot in Leavenworth."

"Probably because you'd been wounded, don't you think?" said the man.

"Exactly," said Charles. "There's men I know, I knew in the band, they never did come back. When it came time to come home in '19 they said to themselves, 'I never had it so good at home,' so they just hid out with some French family, and now I guess they got grandchildren for all I know."

"Don't you ever hear from them?" said the woman.

"I don't want to hear from them," said Charles. "I sowed a few wild oats in Paris. I was a young fellow, and wartime. But I had a family, my wife and in those days the one son. I wanted to get home to my family, settle down, make a future."

"And that's what you did?" she asked.

"Yes, ma'am, that's what I did," said Charles. "Can I mix you another Side Car, ma'am?"

"I guess so," she said.

34

"You, sir? The same?"

"The same," said the man.

They made their way to a table that was as far as any from the bar, They seated themselves and lit cigarettes and smoked in silence, which they did not break when the drinks were served, nor until the sandwiches were brought in by Ira. Even then it was Ira who did the talking; it was apparent that all they wanted to do was wait and think.

They ate their food, and the man ordered a brandy and a Scotch. From the moment they sat down their silence had had its effect, first upon Charles, who created work for himself by rearranging the bottles on the back-bar, and then on Charles and Ira, who found themselves talking in unnaturally lower tones. The quiet of the room was almost total, but not peaceful.

Charles went out to the lobby and when he had got there he called back: "Mr. Studebaker?"

"Yes, Charles?"

"Do you know where's the key to this bottom drawer?"

Ira went to the lobby, frowning until he saw that Charles was holding his finger to his lips.

"Nothing about the key," he murmured. "I just wanted to get you out of there. I think they want to be by themselves."

"I'll go out to the kitchen," said Ira.

In the kitchen Marie Fenstermacher had the day's morning paper spread out on the table in front of her. She was reading the county news. She was leaning slightly forward with her arms folded across her bosom. Ira Studebaker came in and she slowly took off her glasses.

"They like your steak," said Ira.

"Do they want more?" said Marie Fenstermacher.

"I don't guess so, but they put it away, what they had," said Ira.

"The only ones that wouldn't like that steak don't have any teeth, or aren't meat eaters, one or the other."

"It was nicely prepared, though," said Ira.

"I don't have to be told that," she said. "When are you ready for *your* supper?"

"Not for a while yet, I guess. Did you eat?"

"How could I of in that short time? I'm reading the paper till you decide."

"Maybe then you better eat yours, in case some

36

more happen to come in. Charles says there'll be more."

"So he said, but why don't you eat? Does the excitement of two customers ruin your appetite? If it does, this is the wrong business, Mr. Studebaker."

"I guess I am a little excited. I didn't expect customers so soon. We only opened."

She stood up. "Put something in your stomach," she said. "These'll go and on such a night we won't have any more, no matter what Charles is thinking."

"Then if they're going so soon oughtn't I wait and eat in peace? When they go I'll eat with you, if that's all right."

"I'm not so hungry," she said. "I've been picking."

"Picking shouldn't take the appetite away, that's what I understand."

"All I want is a plate of soup and that'll be plenty for me," said Mrs. Fenstermacher.

"Well, then, have your plate of soup with me, when *I* eat. You can be sociable," he said.

"Well, I don't know."

"Sure, you might as well be sociable, the first night we're open."

"The first night, maybe, but remember what I said in the beginning. I'll work for you——"

"Partners," he said.

"Partners. All right. But this sociable stuff— I go home when my work is done, and Rock-bottom won't ever say different. I don't want any funny talk."

"I don't want there to be any, any more than you do," he said.

"They'll talk anyhow, but a respectable woman don't have to worry if there's no truth in it."

"As long as we're in partnership I'll never give them anything to talk about," he said.

"*You* won't? *I* won't, you mean," she said.

"You won't, and I won't," he said. "Well, so."

"So," she said. She put on her glasses and leaned over her paper.

"I'll see if they want any more." He left the kitchen.

In the bar Charles was picking up the horse-back riders' dishes, putting them on a tray. Ira, smiling, said to the man: "Well, everything satisfactory? Did you enjoy your meal?"

"Fine, thanks," said the man. The woman agreed.

"Fine. What else can I get you, like dessert?

38

I can recommend all our pies, all home made right in our own kitchen, if you care for pie. Or——"

"Nothing more to eat, thanks, but I have to ask you a favour," the man said.

"That's what we're here for," said Ira Studebaker.

"Well, wait till you hear what it is, first. You might not be so willing."

Ira smiled. "You want to cash a cheque?"

"Yes."

"That's all right. For how much?"

"Fifty dollars?" said the man.

"Fifty is all right," said Ira. "Do you have your own cheque?"

"No. No cheque and no identification, but. I'll tell you what I'll do. He undid his wrist watch. "You can take my word for it, this watch is worth a damned sight more than fifty dollars. Or ten times fifty dollars."

Ira smiled. "If I didn't think you were honest what good would your watch do me? If you weren't honest the watch could belong to some other person. So if you weren't good for the cheque, all I might get was stolen goods."

The man grinned at the woman. "I must have an honest face."

39

"I never thought so," she said.

"No, you didn't, did you, but apparently Mr. Studebaker thinks so. Mr. Studebaker, I found out your name by asking the man, Charles. My name is Pomfret and I live in New York. H.P. on the back of the watch, that of course doesn't prove anything, but those *are* my initials. Howard Pomfret. That's the closest I have to any identification. My wallet is with my other clothes back at—where I changed. Quite a few miles from here."

"Mr. Pomfrey, you're the one that's talking about identification, not me."

"I know. That's right, isn't it?"

"I may be new in this particular business, but I was in another business for over thirty years, and I didn't go broke, and most of my business had to be done on credit. I'll get you a blank cheque and a pen. If you want to make it for a hundred, that's all right too."

Ira brought the blank cheque and pen to their table. Pomfret began to write. "I have something else to tell you, quite candidly," said Pomfret. "I don't think I'll ever be back this way again, so if you're doing this for good will——"

"I don't *expect* to see you again, you *or* the lady."

"Oh, you don't?" said Pomfret. "Why?"

"Yes, why?" said the woman.

"Well—am I right?"

" You're quite right," she said. " But how do you *know* we won't ever be back?"

"Give a person credit for some intuitions," said Ira.

"You mean that we're not married?" said the woman.

"At first I thought you were, but then I changed my mind."

"What made you change your mind?" she said. "We didn't have that married look?"

"I guess that's it. Or another way to put it, well, two people—you're not kids."

"Say no more, Mr. Studebaker," said the woman, smiling. "Our guilt is written on our faces."

"I didn't say anything about guilt," said Ira.

"I think you may be embarrassing Mr. Studebaker," said Pomfret.

"Or I didn't say I was embarrassed, either," said Ira. He took Pomfret's cheque, glanced at it quickly, tucked it in his vest pocket and from his wallet he drew five ten-dollar bills. "Thank you very much," said Pomfret. "You see, I had two dollars and some change, not enough to get us back to where we have to go. We're almost entirely out of gas. The gauge is just about down to Empty."

Ira frowned. "How far do you have to go? You don't have to tell me where, but how far in miles?"

"I don't know," said Pomfret. "How far would you say, Sweetie?"

"Lord, I don't know. We took so many wrong turns, I'm sure it's over fifty," said the woman.

"The Main Line somewhere? Judging by those clothes," said Ira.

"To the west of the Main Line," said the woman.

"And winding roads," said Ira. "I was in business in Philadelphia before I bought here. I never lived on the Main Line, but we used to go out there for drives. I always had to live in the city because of my business."

"And what was your business, may I ask?" said the woman.

"Oh, that's all right," said Ira. "I doubt if I

42

ever came in contact with your people. Wholesale fruit and produce I was in."

"You may have come in contact with some of my people, as a matter of fact. Some of my family have orchards, and you had to deal with people that owned orchards, didn't you?"

"Personally very seldom, unless they had a big orchard. The ones with big orchards, sometimes it was good business if we arranged to buy a whole crop in advance. Good business for them, good business for us. Sometimes it was poor business. Usually year in, year out, we'd do business with the same people, big and little. If you have an uncle or somebody that had one of the big orchards, maybe I knew him. But only in a business way, ma'am, only in a business way. Half of my life I got up at four o'clock in the morning, that's the way our business works."

"Fascinating," said the woman. "I know I'd love to hear about it some time, but I suppose I never will."

"No, I don't guess you ever will," said Ira. He looked at her a long moment and began to leave them.

"I'm sorry, Mr. Studebaker, ' she said. " I'm sorry I was rude."

"Well—that's all right," he said. "I guess you're worried."

"I am," she said.

"To get back to our original discussion, or one of our original discussions," said Pomfret.

Ira ignored him temporarily. "Worrying won't get you home, ma'am. Let Mr. Pomfrey and I do the worrying," said Ira.

"Well, I am doing some of it, Mr. Studebaker," said Pomfret.

Ira now turned to him. "I know you are," he said. "The first thing to do—is it all right if I sit down?"

Pomfret half rose and Ira took a chair.

"The first thing is the gazzoline," said Ira. "Across the road they got a pump, but a pump locked up is no good. I know this friend of mine that owns the garage. Dewey Kemp. I'll try to get in touch with him." He went to the lobby and dialled two numbers, but he came back to the table shaking his head. "This friend of mine Kemp, that owns the garage, sometimes when he's working on one of his inventions he won't answer the phone. Dewey's an inventor, working on some patent and hates to be interrupted. And a night like tonight, I guess he figures he has a good

44

night to lock up and go home and work on the patent. I know if I happened to be in the garage business I wouldn't expect many customers."

"Possibly not," said Pomfret. "But it's damn poor service. A garage ought to be like a hotel. If *you* weren't open we'd most likely be stuck in the snow somewhere."

"Don't compare me with him. That's the Original Mr. Independent, and you got to admire him for it," said Ira.

"*You* admire him, then," said Pomfret.

"Well, you're pretty independent yourself, Mr. Pomfrey, and I admire that," said Ira, grinning.

"Mr. Studebaker, if you'll take another look at that cheque you so kindly cashed for me, look at the signature. My name is Pomfret. Pom-fret. Not Pomfrey. It's not a hard name."

"Howard, let's you and I stop being surly with this really nice man. He's trying to help us, and the fact of the matter *is*, without his help and kindness we are in a very, very, *very* nasty little *jam*. Will you get that through your arrogant skull?"

"You handle it," said Pomfret.

"All right, I will," she said. "Mr. Studebaker, it's absolutely necessary that we get back to my

45

house before at the latest eleven or eleven-thirty tonight."

"Oh, that you ought to be able to do, providing the roads aren't all too thick with snow. I don't think it's blowing too hard, so it shouldn't be piled up too much."

"I hope you're right," she said. "Now how do we go?"

"Well," said Ira, rubbing his hand over his belly, "the way I'd go would be take that road that intersects us here at the corner and head for Wheelwright. Mind now, it's a country road and maybe it's piled up, but we can find out if it's passable and if it is, that's the way to go. At Wheelwright you'll come to 335 and if you stay on 335 that'll take you in to Norristown."

"I know the way from Norristown," she said. "So it's as simple as that? I wonder where we went wrong?"

"I could answer that question but it wouldn't have anything to do with highways," said Pomfret. Her eyes twinkled but she pretended to ignore his joke. " And if the road isn't clear to Wheelwright, then which way?"

"Then go back the way you came, I mean go east on the Dieglersville road but don't go all the

46

way into Dieglersville. Turn right about a half-mile before Dieglersville and take the road marked Doylestown, but only stay on that road till you meet 335, the same road you'd get to by Wheelwright only by Dieglersville is about fourteen miles longer out of your way."

"Will you write it down for us please?" she said.

Ira got some stationery from the lobby and came back to the table. "I'll write the directions and, yes, I'll draw you a rough map. I'll just put down the principal places to remember, because once you're on 335 you're on your way home."

He had a matching pen and pencil set in his vest pocket. He took them both out together. "These were a present from my drivers and helpers when I sold out to my partner. I like to show them. I kind of expected a *little* something from the people in the office, and they gave me a humidor I have upstairs. But from the drivers and helpers, they used to give me a lot of trouble —I won't say a lot, but, *yes*, a *lot*—they went out on strike on me three times and cost me a lot of money. But the day before I was leaving for good they all came in my office and they gave me this pen and pencil set. They didn't have to

47

do anything for me. I was touched. There for a minute I couldn't think of anything to say. But they couldn't either, and then we all started talking at once—O'Leary, the one they picked to deliver the presentation speech, and I. Both of us started talking at once."

"What did O'Leary say? I'd like to hear," she said.

"Well, I don't know as I ought—it was so complimentary."

"Naturally," she said.

"Well, to the effect that even if we had our differences at least I was always fair and square. They wished me luck in the future. That was when I wasn't sure I was going in the hotel business. Maybe I was sure down deep, but I was letting on I was just retiring."

"By the way, what made you go into the hotel business?" she said.

"Oh, that's a long story," said Ira. "I could make it short for you but first I'll see about gazzoline. There's Charles. Charles, see what my friends will have to drink while I start telephoning again."

The flash blizzard was particularly bad in that

part of Pennsylvania because it is not the part
that usually gets a heavy fall of snow. Thirty
miles to the north, in the mountains, they were
prepared and equipped to deal with the white
stuff in quantity from November until April.
But around Rockbottom, no. In the mountains
there are fewer roads; around Rockbottom, which
is rolling farmland, they have been building roads
for close to three centuries. Sometimes a four-
lane or six-lane highway will parallel a perfectly
good hard-surface road that was built only thirty
or forty years ago and is still used by local traffic,
and the two-lane and six-lane roads will be crossed
or tunnelled by county roads that were feeders
when long-distance travel was by stagecoach
and Conestoga wagon, although the Conestoga
wagons were more popular to the south and
south-west. An accurate and complete road map
of some of the counties around Macungie (and
Macungie itself) would make a stranger wonder
how the farmers ever got any farming done, what
with so many roads and paths and trails. But the
farmers had solved that for themselves, in many
cases, by simply deciding that such-and-such a
road wasn't any use any more, and ploughing it
up and cultivating it. But on the other hand

49

and lit their cigarettes. "He's a funny little old guy," said Pomfret.

"If I'm not mistaken he's the same age as Alex, give or take a year," she said.

"How old *is* Alex, anyway?" said Pomfret.

" Fifty-five," she said.

"Yeah, I guess so."

"I know so. He's sixteen years older than I am," she said.

"No, I meant Alex was about the same age as this fellow. Studebaker gives you the impression of being older, but I don't suppose he is."

"It's the clothes," she said. " Alex always in country clothes, and no lines in his face. When did you ever see Alex when he wasn't sunburned?"

"Never, I guess," said Pomfret.

"Good food, outdoor life, nothing to worry about," she said.

"Nothing to worry about?" said Pomfret.

"Well—no, nothing to worry about," she said. "Not so far. The only thing that'll bother him is if people say I just nipped off with you. I'd be satisfied to protect his pride."

"So would I," said Pomfret. " In fact, isn't that what we're worrying about now?"

"Yes," she said.

51

"Here we sit, sweating it out in a place called Rockbottom, P A, because we want to protect Alex's pride."

"Well, more than that," she said. "Fear."

"Well, yes, because you don't want him to take Esther away from you. But that's protecting his pride. If his pride weren't affected he'd probably be reasonable about sharing Esther."

"I don't want him to share her. I don't want him to have anything to do with bringing her up. I've fought it all her life and I don't want to see her spoiled now. This'd be just the time, too. Just the time he could spoil her. You don't know what that much money can do."

"No, but I'd be willing to learn," said Pomfret.

She passed over his remark. "I saw it happen, a girl I know tried to bring up not one but *two* daughters in the present day and not Mr. Stotesbury's era. No relation of Mr. Stotesbury's, just using him as a symbol. What happened? She and her husband parted company and he didn't even get custody, but he began it, very subtly, lots of little presents, then bigger presents, trips abroad, 21, El Morocco. Well, one of those girls is only a year older than Esther, but she's pregnant and getting a divorce. The older sister, twenty-three years old, she's divorced and living with an actor that has a wife and a couple of children. And all because the father blinded them with money. They were *wonderful* kids, lovely."

"What about the mother?" said Pomfret.

"A drunk. A falling-down hopeless alcoholic."

"Is she married again?" said Pomfret.

"Heavens no. All puffed out, lost every *vestige* of her looks, plays around with a bunch of pansies in New York."

"Who is it, do I know her?"

"Kitty George, I guess you've probably met her."

"I saw her last week at a dinner party," said Pomfret. "I hardly recognized her, not that I ever knew her very well."

"It could happen to me," she said.

"Not to you, Martha," he said. He put his hand on hers.

"It might. It could," she said. "Nobody ever thought it could happen to Kitty, either. But it did. It did."

"It won't happen to you," he repeated.

"This could be where it begins to happen to me. I *have* to get Eleanor. She's my best friend, one I can trust. I *have* to talk to her before Alex talks to her. Alex, you know, he's liable to call her and just casually ask to speak to me, and she's liable to just answer without thinking, 'She's not here.' And there goes the apple cart. He'll ask himself where else I could have gone, and there isn't any place else really, not without leaving word."

"He never kept such careful tabs on you," said Pomfret. "You've spent how many nights in New York and he never bothered to check up on you."

"Oh, this isn't only the jealous husband. This is the solicitous husband. The blizzard. For a man about town, darling, I can't say you think of everything. For instance, Alex knows by this time that the horses were vanned back and comfortably munching their hay, right this minute. He knows Graybar is back at Eleanor's—that's the name of the horse you had, in case you forgot. Well, the horses are snug for the night, but the station wagon is missing, and I'm missing with it, and it wouldn't take long for him to find out you're missing too, if he wanted to put his mind to it. Two and two together, or just two together, you and I. Tell that man I'd like another drink will you?"

"Charles!" he called. "Could you do this again, please?"

"Yes, sir," said Charles.

"While he's bringing the drinks I'll try Eleanor again. Give me some change, please."

She was gone between five and ten minutes, and when she came back her face was calm, but before she spoke she drank a full pony of brandy and lit a cigarette.

"And?" he said.

"Alex called twice. The first time Eleanor said— luckily, pure luck—I hadn't gotten there *yet*. Not that she was expecting me. She just happened to put in 'yet.' So he told her he heard on the radio or somewhere that there was a blizzard on the way, and I wasn't to stay too long at her house, or I'd have to spend the night. Well, Eleanor's my friend."

"Does she know about us?"

"Yes, or at least what I haven't told her she's guessed," said Martha. " But then he called again about two hours later and wanted to speak to me, of course, and Eleanor, trying to stall him off, said she was definitely expecting me but I hadn't arrived. 'Well, I don't know,' he said. 'I've given Martha plenty of time to get to your

55

house. I think I'll have the police scour the neighbourhood. She may be off in a ditch somewhere, cracked up.' "

"Oh, Christ. The cops," said Pomfret.

"So that's where it is now."

"Did Eleanor think he sounded suspicious?"

"Mystified, more than suspicious. Just couldn't understand it all."

"What did you tell Eleanor?"

"The truth," said Martha. "The essential facts. That I was with you, that we drove and talked and drove and talked till we got lost and landed here." She smiled.

"What's funny?" he asked.

"Eleanor. She has a good dirty mind. She said we couldn't have had much fun if we were both wearing riding breeches."

"Hmm."

She looked at him, into his eyes, to his mouth, into his eyes again. " I want to touch you. I want you to touch me," she said.

He smiled. "I'm way ahead of you, sweetheart."

"This would have been a wonderful place, too," she said. "I'll bet they have big old four-poster beds. I'd like to spend a week-end here, wouldn't you?"

56

"Yes," he said. "just about this time of the year. Have the maid come in and close the window and serve us breakfast."

"Not in bed, though. I don't like breakfast in bed."

"No, but a cup of coffee in bed," he said.

"That'd be all right. Then breakfast in our dressing gowns."

"Then we'd decide what to do that day. Go for a walk and see the sights."

"I don't imagine that'd take very long," she said.

"I wouldn't want it to. Just a short stroll, then back to the hay."

"Aren't you exaggerating your prowess?" she said. "We just got up, and after the night before, at least I hope after the night before. . . ."

"Maybe you're right. I need a little more rest. We could both rest. Maybe no stroll. Just back to bed after breakfast and rest till lunch."

"Lunch in our room?"

"I'm beginning to think we wouldn't leave the room at all. Spend the whole week-end there," he said.

"Have you ever done that?"

"Yes, in Atlantic City."

"You didn't have to answer so quickly," she said. " You might have pretended to give it a moment's thought."

"After a moment's thought, yes, in Atlantic City, I think it was, or Coney Island, it might have been. Or maybe it was the Ritz Hotel in Paris. Maybe I never did."

"Thank you," she said. "But the fact is, you did, in Atlantic City. Who was the girl? Not your wife."

"No, not my wife, and not anybody you know, and in *fact*, and I'm telling you the God's honest truth, all I remember is that her name was Betty."

"That's all you remember?"

"Of a statistical nature. One other statistic. I gave her a hundred dollars."

"Oh, a whore."

"Not a regular call-house whore. No, she wasn't a whore. She was kind of a girl around New York, a photographer's model, well paid. I gave her the money because she cancelled a couple of jobs."

"Did you take her picture?"

He laughed. "No, but frankly I thought of it. She was quite a dish."

"Yes, and she was probably used to posing for that kind of a picture, too."

58

"It was so long ago, Girl. I don't want to remember her, I want to be with you. You're my
last love, my final love."

"Why?"

"Because you have a thin nose and sad eyes
and you're the picture of health."

"Sad eyes? Am I supposed to like that?" she
said.

"The way I mean it you are. It was the first
thing I noticed the first time I ever saw you."

"I don't believe *that*," she said. "I remember
the dress I was wearing, and nobody noticed my
eyes in that dress."

"I did, though. You were sitting down and you
had your hands folded in front of you and you
were listening to Joe Lyle sitting next to you.
Like this." He clasped his hands and lowered
his right shoulder and cocked his head like a deaf
person.

"And you thought I had sad eyes."

"I've thought so ever since. Wisdom, tenderness
and sympathy, and love. I didn't know who
you were or anything about you, but I knew
there was love there."

"There is for you. There isn't for anyone else,
but there is for you."

59

"I know," he said. "We haven't got time to fool around with each other."

"No, but I wouldn't give all the rest for the time we *have* got."

He took a deep breath that was a sigh, but a pleasurable one. "Here we are, maybe at the low point of our lives together, but I've never been happier in my life."

They heard a stamping on the lobby floor. Under the swinging door they could see Ira Studebaker knocking the snow from his arctics, and in a few seconds he entered the bar and walked quickly to their table and sat down. He was shaking his head.

"Get your breath first, Mr. Studebaker," said Martha.

He took a couple of breaths, "I'm not used to that," he said. "I wish you folks could stay here for the night."

"But you know—our circumstances," said Martha.

He took another long breath. "Well, I don't know about that. I wouldn't fall over dead with surprise if—whew—if this old hotel . . . Charles, will you bring me a glass of water, please?"

Pomfret and Martha waited patiently, politely.

60

Ira sipped the water and smoothed his thinning locks.

"Well, we can talk about that, later. Now here's the news, some good, some bad. I couldn't rouse him up. Either he's not home, or he turned out all the lights and went to bed. I yelled for him and all, banged on the front door and the kitchen door and even the cellar door. I scraped away some of the snow off the cellar door and stomped my feet, but no answer. No answer at all. So I'm afraid we have to give up trying to get any gazzoline from the pump. But that isn't saying you don't get gazzoline.

"I remembered coming back here, *my* tank is full and we can siphon it out of *my* tank. Ten-fifteen gallons easy, and that'll more than take you past Norristown, and anyway there'll probably be garages open along the way. So there you are."

"Have you got a siphon?" said Pomfret. Charles from behind the bar, spoke up: "Yes, sir, I got one in my car if Mr. Studebaker don't have one in his. I always keep a siphon."

"But one other thing, I wouldn't try to get a hundred feet from here without chains. You couldn't *get* a hundred feet without chains, and between here and Dieglersville you have a steep

61

hill, up one side and down the other, and not too wide a road in case you meet another car coming towards you. What is that car you have out there—and by the way, did you take a look at it since you came in? This much snow all over it."

"It's a Buick station wagon," said Martha.

"Then I think my chains'll fit your tyres. I have an Oldsmobile, a '49."

"It's a '49 station wagon," said Martha.

"I should think you'd have owned a Studebaker," said Pomfret.

"Oh, I guess we're related 'way back, but I always preferred a bigger car if I could afford it. Or rather Irma, Mrs. Studebaker, she did, and I took delivery of this car before she passed away. Although on the farm we had a Studebaker wagon in those days. They're of course Indiana people and I don't remember whether my father ever said we were or weren't related."

"Well then, I guess we're all set," said Pomfret. "If Charles will give me a hand I'll get some gas in my tank and put on the chains." He stood up. "There's no use my even trying to thank you, Mr. Studebaker."

"But try," said Martha.

62

"No, I won't, but maybe you can," said Pomfret.

Ira smiled. "Nobody has to thank me," he said. "I used to read those ads about the Statler hotels. You know, how they hold a train for somebody, or send a bellboy with a man's false teeth when he forgot them and went to a banquet at some other hotel. You know those ads. Well, that's hotel service, and we want to do as good."

"Except that we'll never be back," said Pomfret.

"We might," said Martha. "Some day."

Pomfret nodded slowly, then abruptly picked up his hat and coat and went out with Charles.

There was quiet between Ira and Martha, quiet and not an uneasy silence. Then she spoke: "I'm a married woman and I'm in love with him. I have a young daughter, and I don't want to let her father bring her up. Not that her father isn't a good man. He's a good man, kind and generous. But I want my daughter brought up to realize that this is 1950. If my husband brought her up—he's very rich, and he doesn't like what's going on in the world. He hasn't changed any since Coolidge was President."

"How is the little girl now? How old is she?"

said Ira. They were not looking at each other. He sat with his elbows on the table and his hands clasped. She sat with her hands in her lap, leaning slightly forward and seeming to be addressing the top of the table.

"She's eighteen and very sweet and bright, but she's still young enough to be impressionable. She adores her father and she likes me too. We're very good friends, as much as mother and daughter."

"Did you ever stop to think that some of the niceness she has—some of that could be her father too? You can't even make yourself say something against him, so maybe—I don't know."

"How many children have you got, Mr. Studebaker?"

"None. We lost the one, and my wife had to have her tubes out. How many does Mr. Pomfret have?"

"Three. Two girls and a boy. The oldest girl's the same age as my daughter, then a girl sixteen and a boy eleven or twelve. They're with their mother. He's been divorced about three years."

"On account of you?"

"Before I met him," said Martha.

"It's quite a situation," said Ira.

"Up at Yale," said Martha.

"What?"

"Nothing," she said. A short silence, then "You were going to tell me about the hotel, how you happened to buy it. I think we're on safer ground there."

"Yes. Well, I buried Irma on the tenth day of January, this year. She'd been very poorly for a number of years. When she had her tubes out that was a long time ago, and modern science didn't know as much about cancer as they do now. Then she had the one breast removed, and I'll tell you, Mrs.— say, I don't know your name, I'll call you Mrs. Pomfret."

"My name is Paul. Mrs. Alexander Paul. My first name is Martha."

"Martha. I'd rather call you Martha. Well, so Irma lingered on, but it was a merciful thing for her when she died. I'd like to have a dollar for every time I was tempted to give her an overdose of some dope and end her suffering. But she knew what I was thinking. She said to me more than once. 'Ira,' she'd say, that sweet smile of hers on her face, 'I know what you're thinking,' she'd say. 'But don't do it. I could do it myself, or we could do it together, but

65

I'm happy being with you,' she'd say, 'and
if we took our own lives—we're not sure. Here
we're together, and we're sure of this.' Then I'd
be the one that would cry like a baby, and all the
time she was the one in pain. So I buried her on
the tenth day of January.

"One thing they did know, they knew when
she was gonna die. They told me, and I began
making preparations for selling out to my partner
and getting away from Philadelphia. I told my
partner, I said when Irma died I didn't want to
be in Philadelphia any more. Too full of memories.

"But then what did I do? I brought Irma back
here to Rockbottom, to the family plot. I was from
here too. Both of us were. Married here, that
church across the way there. And courted here
and except when I was with the Reading for a
year, before I went into the fruit and produce
business, and the one year I was at Normal, we
spent all our lives either here or in Philadelphia.
We only ever lived in but three houses all our
married life, married in '17.

"Well, there were one or two things to clean
up here and I stayed over in the hotel in Dieglersville, but I noticed this old place and in the back
of my mind I always used to do business with hotel

people, and I liked hotels. We went to Atlantic every year and I was always asking questions about the hotel business, so it was always in the back of my mind. And so I decided to look into the old Farmers. This old place. Well, the bank was only too willing to let me take it off their hands and put my own money into it. My partner thought I was crazy with grief when I told him what I was doing. He told me to take a rest and all, and when I told him I was going through with the deal, this deal, he said, well, if I lost my money he'd always offer me a job with the old business. I don't know, maybe I'll be back selling bananas in a year or so, but a man ought to keep himself occupied. And here I can remember Irma more when she wasn't suffering. It's funny, I *think* of her all the time here, but I'm getting away from some of those days when she had to scream with the pain, when the nurse didn't give her the stuff in time. I'm getting away from that and more remembering her as a young girl.

"Well, that's how I got in this business. I got Marie Fenstermacher, her uncle used to own this place years ago and she tried to make a go of it but didn't want to sell liquor, so I got her to come in as a partner to do the real work. Then I inquired around among the hotel and club men I knew and heard about Charles, Charles Mannering, so I signed him up. He was with one of the society clubs in Philadelphia and before that Baltimore and before that, God knows. I can just sit and listen to Charles by the hour.

"I don't know, I put over a hundred and twenty thousand in this place, the way you see it now. I tried to make it as much like the old-time farmers' hotels they used to have in this part of the country. I'm doing a little advertising to attract the chicken-and-waffle trade, and give everybody their money's worth. I put in Beauty-rest mattresses and a few things like that. Plumbing. Pretty good plumbing was in. All brass pipes, you know. Marie Fenstermacher's uncle spent a small fortune on the place before he passed away. I think he had the understanding they were going to put a main road through here, but where he got his information from, they were wrong.

"You ought to take a look around and see how this place is built. No nails in the timbering. All pegs. Joists eighteen inches thick, you know."

"Really?" said Martha.

He laughed. "Oh, Lord," he said. "My Lord, Martha, this is the longest I've talked since I don't know how long. I guess I've been on the listening end with Charles so long, when I got a polite listener myself I sure let go with both barrels. It's a wonder you're not half asleep.

"Say, let me get you a nice cup of coffee. You're going to want a cup of coffee before you go out in that snow, and I'll have some ready when Mr. Pomfret gets back."

"I would like a cup of coffee," she said.

He got up, robbing his vest. "One thing I don't have," he said. "I wish I had a thermos bottle I could let you take with you. That would have been just the ticket, you know. We may have some kind of a Mason jar or something like that I could fill with hot coffee. It ought to keep pretty warm. Or maybe an empty liquor bottle. Or maybe Charles'll have some ideas. We'll ask him when they get back. But now, I'd kind of like a cup of coffee myself. I'll be back in a jiffy. Cream and sugar? Well, I'll bring 'em anyway."

He went out and Martha got up and walked around the room, purposelessly, ending up by standing at the bar and gazing at her reflection

69

in the back-bar mirror. She stopped that suddenly and went to the telephone booth, where she remained for five minutes. When she came out she was half smiling. She returned to her table to wait for Howard Pomfret.

She was sitting back relaxed in her chair and felt the draught from the front door opening.

"Tillers of the soil! I say there, tillers of the soil! My good host!" someone called.

The voice was a man's, and not Howard's and certainly not the voice of Mr. Studebaker or Charles Mannering.

The bar door swung open and a little man stepped inside the bar, glanced about till he saw Martha. "Well, *say*," he said. He was below medium height, with a sharp, intelligent face and large brown eyes. He was wearing a chocolate-coloured polo coat with a buckle-less belt, brown pork-pie hat, soaking wet brown suede shoes. He grinned at Martha and she grinned back. "Well, say now," he said. He gave her costume a quick look. "Tillers of the soil my—are we in time for the stirrup cup, old dear? Did we have good hunt-ting? Tally-ho!"

"Tally-ho yourself," said Martha amiably.

He walked over to her table, removing the

70

snowed-on hat. "My name is Jerry Mayo," he said.

"Is it?" she said.

"Oh, now, that's no way to be, Consuelo," he said. "It *is Consuelo*, isn't it?" He was putting on a comedy English accent.

"Suit yourself," said Martha.

"You know, I never saw one of you people close to," he said. "This isn't an act, is it? You are the genuine huntin', shootin', aren't you?"

"The genuine," she said.

"You really *wear* those, uh, Ascots and stuff."

"It's called a stock," she said.

"Well, it's very becoming, on you. But you could wear an old empty cement bag and you'd do things for it," he said. "God was good to you."

"Thank you, Mr. Mayo," she said.

"Ahh, she remembered the name," he said.

"I once owned a horse from the County Mayo," she said.

"Well, I been compared to a horse, one end of it," he said. He sat down at her table. "Tell me, what's the pitch here? Is this a private club or what? It has a sign out, hotel, but you, you got me wondering whether it's a hotel or what."

"It's a hotel, just opened today, in fact. Or re-opened."

"Oh, I catch. And they invited the gentry for the premeer."

"No, I'm here by accident, the same as you," she said.

"Jesus Christ, I hope your luck is better than ours," he said. He offered her a Camel, which she refused, and he shook the pack until a single cigarette popped up and he stuck the cigarette in a corner of his mouth without first taking it out of the pack. He took a kitchen match from the holder on the table and scratched it with a thumb-nail. He did not blow it out; he shook it out with two snappy shakes.

"Well, that depends," she said.

"Are you alone?"

She smiled. "Are you trying to move in?" she said. "Don't think I wouldn't like to," he said. "I'm not much bigger than a jockey, but I understand some of them do all right with you huntin'-shootin's."

"Not that I ever heard of," she said.

"Well, I didn't either," he said. "But I like to think the worst. 'I'll win this race for you, Miss

Whitney, but under one condition.' You know what I mean?"

"Yes, I know what you mean," she said.

"You're pretty *hip* for your set," he said.

"They're not all stupid," she said.

"I got no way of knowing," he said. "Outside of the way they look when they have their pictures taken. 'Miss De*borah* Debutante.' She'd look better with a bit in her mouth. 'Mr. and Mrs. J. Tonsil Adenoids at the El Morocco.' Don't they have enough moo to keep those pictures out of the papers? They cause more Communists than Stalin."

"I won't argue with you," she said.

"You know what I mean," he said. "Who wants money if that's what it does to you?"

"Absolutely. I couldn't agree more whole-heartedly," she said.

"It puts the knock on the capitalistic system," he continued. "As the big boys say, no incentive."

"Absolutely," she said.

"Well, Connie," he said. "This is delightful and all that sort of pip-pip, but where are the peasants that run this flea-bag? I got two freezing broads out in that heap of mine. Two more

73

minutes and they won't thaw out till Spring, and we got work to do."

"You ought to bring them in," she said. "There'll be hot coffee here in a minute or two."

"Done and done," he said. He went out and in a minute he was back again, accompanying two shivering girls who were dressed alike in short dyed-muskrat coats, open-toed platform shoes and Truman-type caps. The clothes, alike even to the ravages inflicted on them by the weather, and the girls' make-up—Joan Craw-fordish mouths, Hedy Lamarrish eyebrow plucks —only helped to bring out the lack of real resemblance between the girls; instead of looking like twins they did not even look like sisters, and one of them was obviously at least five years older than the other. They were carrying identical weekend bags, tired little satchels of striped canvas with stickers from a very minor airline.

"Connie, it gives me pleasure to present the Pickwick Sisters. This is Conchita and this is Paulette," he said. "Pickwicks, this is Connie, no last name."

Paulette, the older, muttered: "Acquaintance."

Conchita, " I'm sure."

74

"Won't you sit down?" said Martha. "The proprietor's getting some hot coffee."

The girls sat stiffly, without opening their coats. They folded their hands in their laps and stared at Martha.

"Are you lost too?" said Martha.

They looked at Mayo, like saying: "That's your department."

"You had to be lost to get to this place," he said to Martha. "The first early settlers must of got lost. Which way you headed, Pardner?"

". . . Norristown," said Martha.

"I never heard of it. Is it far?" said Mayo.

"About fifty miles," said Martha. She tried to include the Pickwicks in her question: "How far off do you think you are?"

"I got news for you," said Mayo. "These dreams are lost on Twelfth Avenya, and they were born on Eleventh."

"Oh, is that so?" said Paulette.

"Is that so?" said Conchita.

"Answering your question," said Mayo. "Reading, P A, is where we were headed, and where we gotta be by eleven. Ah, here's our smiling host wit' the mocha-java." He stood up as Ira walked in with a tray and the coffee things. "Could you do that again, Sport? Three more cups? And three ham on rye."

Ira paid no attention to him until he had poured a cup of coffee for Martha. He took a quick look at the girls and then spoke to Mayo: "What can I do for you?"

"The scoff, and then show us how to get to Reading, P A."

"The scarf? What scarf?" said Ira.

Mayo turned to Martha; "He doesn't dig me," then, to Ira Studebaker: "Not scarf, around your neck; scoff, down the throat. Eatin' material. We want three cups of coffee and three ham on rye. Go on, Dad, get the lead out."

No one ever had spoken to Ira like that in his entire life, and Ira never had spoken to anyone like Jerry Mayo. Ira did not get cross. Jerry Mayo was so foreign to him that there was not even common ground for offence. "With mustard?" said Ira.

"With mustard to be sure," said Jerry. "With mustard, cream and sugar, salt and pepper, a couple slices of dill pickle. The works. The schmeer."

Ira shook his head, smiled at Martha (whose casual manner with Jerry and the Pickwicks

76

mystified him), and departed for the kitchen.

"Where's the facilities?" said Jerry to Martha. "I see the boys', but I don't see the girls'."

"Oh," said Martha. "Up the stairs in the lobby, the first landing."

He spoke to the girls. "Well, Picksies," he said. "You heard the lady. Out there and up the steps. Do I have to lift you on?"

"*Oh*," they said. They rose and walked out in step.

"I'm 'uman too," said Jerry, going to the men's room.

Martha was alone not long. Howard Pomfret returned and it was plain to see that something was wrong. Her smile disappeared as he ignored her outstretched hand. "All set?" she said.

"I can't start the god-damn thing," he said. He unbuttoned his coat, sat down and lit a cigarette, tossed his hat on a chair. "We siphoned off about ten gallons of gas, then the God-damn thing wouldn't turn over. It's not the battery. It's probably the distributor. It isn't frozen. Charles thinks it's the distributor . . . What were you all happy-face about?"

"I called Eleanor again," said Martha. "Twice. She called Alex and told him I was at her house, passed out."

"Did *that* work?"

"Like a charm. She said he laughed. He said he *knew* that was what happened. He said he knew it all along. He knew she was just trying to protect me."

"What if he goes to her house?"

"That's the chance we take, but you don't know Alex. He runs from drunks like I don't know what. He'll drink all day and all night and never get tight, but let someone get the least bit gassed and he won't go near them. Especially a female."

"That must restrict his activities, from what I've seen of some of your friends."

"As long as they don't get tight," she said. "So I was happy-face because now it doesn't make any difference when I get home. He's gone to bed, and in the morning I'll pretend I have a hangover and all will be well. He'll be amused and superior."

"Well, fine, but we have to get home some time," said Pomfret.

Jerry Mayo came out of the men's room. Pomfret looked at him, one quick look, and turned away, not so much contemptuously as with disdain. He shrank back as from a serpent when

78

Jerry came to him and said: "Mayo's the name. Jerry Mayo."

"Mr. Mayo's been entertaining me while you were gone," said Martha.

"He has? How?" Howard stared incredulously as Mayo seated himself at their table.

"Just a voice from another world," said Mayo. "Fellow castaways on life's shores, to meet and then pass on."

"Who the hell *is* this?" said Howard.

"It's Mr. Mayo. He's travelling with two young ladies on their way to Reading," said Martha. "I gather they're in the theatrical business. Just a guess, of course." She smiled at Mayo.

"Oh, I suppose he owns that sedan across the street," said Howard.

"Owns is quite a big word, but yes, it is his car," said Jerry. "He doesn't want to bother anybody, so he'll sit over there if he's spoiling anybody's supper." He sneered at Howard and started to rise.

"No, no, sit down, Mr. Mayo," said Martha.

"I'm not sticking my nose in where I'm not wanted," said Jerry.

"Well, if you expect me to say I can't live without you, guess again," said Howard.

79

"Who writes your dialogue?" said Jerry.

"Oh, stop it!" said Martha. "Grow up. Both of you."

Jerry grinned at her. "Who writes *your* dialogue, Con?"

The Pickwicks re-entered the bar, still in step. "The Misses Pickwick, this is Mr. Pomfret."

"Acquaintance," said Paulette, the older.

"I'm sure," said Conchita.

Reluctantly Howard got to his feet and stood, not quite erect, while they took chairs and folded their hands in their laps. He acknowledged the introduction with a nod, glaring at Martha for mentioning his name.

"I was just guessing," said Martha to the Pickwicks. "I made a guess that you're in the theatrical business."

They looked at Jerry, turning the question over to him.

"Well—yes," he said. "Yes. We're in show business. Not Noel Coward kind of show business. Say, uh, Billboard kind of show business."

They all watched as Ira brought the sandwiches and coffee.

"Everything okay, Mr. Pomfret?" said Ira.

"Got the gas in the car, but now it won't turn

over. Charles thinks it's the distributor. It may be the starter."

"Then you couldn't get the chains on?" said Ira.

"No. We could have pushed it, I guess, but what's the use?" said Pomfret. "I wonder if I could have a cup of coffee."

"Take mine," said Conchita.

"Take mine," said Paulette.

"You're in, brother," said Jerry.

"Am I, brother?" said Howard.

"I got news for you," said Jerry. "I never saw them offer anybody anything to eat ever since I knew them. You *must* be in."

"Care for half of my sandwich?" said Conchita.

"Ma'am, would you care for half of mine?" said Paulette to Martha.

Jerry lifted his plate and placed it before Martha.

"We've had dinner, thanks," she said. "But thanks ever so much."

"I'll get you a cup of coffee," said Ira to Pomfret.

"Say, I never introduced you to the Pickwicks," said Jerry, "Conchita Pickwick and Paulette Pickwick, this is Mr. Farmers."

81

"Mr. Studebaker," said Martha.

"Glad to meet you," said Ira.

"Acquaintance," said Paulette.

"I'm sure," said Conchita.

"I'll get the coffee," said Ira.

Dr. J. Henry Graeff came in. "Folks, this is Doctor Graeff. You all introduce yourselves." He left.

"Good evening, good evening," said Dr. Graeff.

"Heavenly days, it's Doctor Gamble," said Jerry.

The doctor frowned at Jerry. He walked over to the group, taking off his hat and coat and laying them on a chair. "Well, some weather."

Jerry leaned over and whispered to Martha: "I wonder who writes *his* dialogue?" Aloud he said: "'Tain't a fit night out for man nor beast."

"W. C. Fields," said Pomfret.

"Oh. Oho," said Jerry. "He's *quick*."

"Anybody care for a little something stronger than coffee?" said Dr. Graeff.

Jerry spoke: "This guy went into a saloon and his horse was with him. He said to the bartender, 'Give my horse a bucketful of whisky.' So the bartender poured a couple of quarts of whisky into the bucket, and the horse drank it. 'Fill it

82

up again,' said the fellow. So the bartender filled it up again and the horse drank it. 'How much is that?' the fellow said. 'That'll be twenty dollars,' said the bartender. 'How about you having a drink on the house?' 'Me? Not *me*,' the fellow said. '*I'm driving!*' "

The Pickwicks tittered, Dr. Graeff laughed, and Martha smiled. Jerry looked at each in turn and when he came to Howard he saw he was not amused. "The fellow said, '*I'm driving!*' " Jerry repeated, as to a not-bright child.

"I heard you," said Howard Pomfret. "I also heard the story. Two years ago."

"I got news for you," said Jerry. "Two years old is brand-new for one of my stories."

"If you'll excuse me—" said Howard. To Martha he said: "I'm going out and see how he's coming along." They all watched his departure as though it were an event of great importance, but really they watched only to have something to do. Watching him, listening to the talk, the Pickwicks let nothing interfere with their ritualistic eating: each of the girls sat with the right hand lying palm up in her lap and held the half-sandwich in the left hand. She would raise the sandwich to her mouth, take a nibble, and begin

to chew with quick deep bites. Then after swallow-
ing the food she would take a mouthful of coffee,
swallow it, put the hand back on the lap, raise
the left hand with the sandwich. There was nothing
especially remarkable about their eating except
that the motions were identical and almost simulta-
neous; Paulette would make one of the motions,
and Conchita would duplicate it a second later.

"Business looks pretty good for the first night,"
said the doctor. "You know this is the first night
this place's been open. At least in several years.
I hope it's a good sign."

"I hope so," said Martha.

"How's doctoring?" said Jerry.

"Oh, that doesn't change much," said the
doctor.

"I guess they won't be cracking their skulls
till tomorrow, eh, Doc? Slipping on the ice?" said
Jerry.

"No, I don't suppose so," said the doctor.
"You folks care for a snifter?"

"Well, I gave you my answer. That egg I laid,
that story. I'm driving. And I don't think the
Picks want anything. We have to work tonight.
if we ever get out of this whistle-stop. Say, Doc,
how do you get to Reading?"

The doctor seemed to be reflecting. "Well, by dog-sled, tonight," he said.

"Uh-huh," said Jerry. "Now you laid *your* egg. I'll feed you another straight line. I'm sittin' here, you're sittin' there, and I say to you, Doc, how do we get to Reading. Only this time, how about a straight answer?"

The answer was not given. There was a pounding on the door at the side of the room opposite the lobby side. They all turned in the direction of the pounding, and Dr. Graeff got up. "I guess Ira didn't open that door."

He turned the key and admitted a man in truck-driver's uniform. He was six feet tall and weighed close to two hundred. He glanced over at the group and then walked to the bar, turning his back on the others. He waited and then said to the doctor: "Well, don't I get no service?"

"I'm not the bartender," said the doctor, "but I guess I can wait on you. What can I get you?"

"Rye. Water on the side," said the truckman.

The doctor picked out a bottle of rye and put it on the bar and ran a glass of water, putting it and a shot glass beside the rye. The man helped himself and downed the drink and took a sip of water. He poured another rye and drank it. "Who owns that God-damn Buick? One of *them?*" he asked the doctor.

"I do," said Martha.

"You'll have to get it out of the way," said the truckman. "I can't get by with that thing there."

"That's what they're trying to do," said Martha. "But you needn't be so tough about it."

"Who's tryin' to get it out of the way? I didn't see nobody tryin' to get it out."

"Well, take another look, because there are *two* people trying to start it. There's something the matter with the distributor."

"It don't take two people to fix no distributor," he said.

"Why don't *you* try it, then?" said Martha.

"Yes, why don't you try it?" said Paulette.

"Yes," said Conchita.

"Who the hell asked you for your advice?" he said to the Pickwicks.

"If you can start the car we'll be only too glad to get out of your way," said Martha. "Besides, I don't think we *are* in your way."

"Go out and take a look," said the truckman. "*You* take a look. Take a look at my truck. It

86

makes three of your God-damn Buick. Gimme another shot."

"Help yourself," said the doctor.

"I got a load of milk——"

"You'll have another load in a minute, not milk, either," said Jerry.

"Oh, a wise guy," said the truckman. He put down the bottle and shot glass and sauntered over to the table.

"Don't you touch him!" cried Paulette.

"Don't you dare touch him!" said Conchita.

The truckman grinned and reached down and flipped Jerry's tie so that it slapped against his face.

"Oh, stop it, you big bully," said Martha. "Go on, get out of here."

"You got a necktie on too," said the truckman.

"You touch me and I'll brain you with this ketchup bottle," said Martha.

The doctor came from behind the bar. "Cut it out," he said. "If you create a disturbance in here I'll call the state police. Now get about your business and leave these people alone. Go on, now."

The truckman grinned at them and then returned to the bar. He poured another rye and drank it. The room was all a heavy silence. Then Martha spoke: "Why don't you be nice and see if *you* can start my car?"

"You wanted to hit me with the bottle of ketchup," said the truckman, grinning.

"I'm sorry about that, but please go on and see if you can get my car started. *You* want to get away as much as we do."

He said nothing, but he was thinking it over, or thinking something over, and while he was thinking a state highway patrolman entered from the door the truckman had used.

The patrolman took off his gauntlets. "Hello, Doc," he said. "All these people stuck?"

"Hello, Corporal," said the doctor. "Yes, they are."

The truckman watched the doctor.

"Is that your truck out there?" said the corporal.

"Yeah," said the truckman.

"Well, get moving, you're blocking the road," said the corporal.

"I can't get by that Buick," said the truckman, still eyeing the doctor.

"It's my Buick, Corporal," said Martha. "He's going to help get it started."

"What's the matter with it?" said the corporal.

"It won't start."

"I gathered that," said the corporal. "Is the battery dead?"

"I don't know," said Martha.

"Well, you're not gonna find out sitting here," said the corporal. "Let's take a look at it."

"My husband and the man that works here are trying to get it started," said Martha.

"I didn't see anybody trying to get it started," said the corporal. "There's nobody out there."

"Well, I can't imagine where they went," said Martha.

Ira Studebaker came in. "Oh, hello, Corporal," he said.

"Hello, Mr. Studebaker. You got a bunch of refugees here. Good for business, huh?"

"Yes, so it seems," said Ira. "Can I get you a cup of coffee or anything?"

"No, thanks," said the corporal. "I just want to get this fellow with the truck out of the way, and you got this station wagon stuck, I understand."

"They're fixing it. They took something off the engine and they're back in my garage trying to fix it," said Ira.

"Sure it isn't the battery?" said the corporal.

89

"They're sure of that," said Ira. "They think it's the distributor, but I wouldn't know."

"Why don't *you* go out and help them?" said the corporal to the truckman. "And lay off that booze with that big truck. I could turn you in."

"I just wanted to warm up," said the truckman.

"Yeah. Warm up and fall asleep," said the corporal. "You lay off that and see if you can give these people a hand. Go on, beat it."

"You didn't happen to see if Dewey Kemp's light was on?" said Ira.

"We came the other way, but Dewey's in Allentown. I know that for sure. If you can't get the Buick started, call the sub-station and leave a message and maybe I can get somebody from Dieglersville. But this fellow ought to be able to fix it, whatever it is. Well, what are you waiting for? Go on out and give those people a hand."

The truckman left by the lobby door.

"Which way are you headed, Lady?" said the corporal to Martha.

"Well, Norristown," she said.

"Go by Dieglersville," said the corporal. "The Wheelwright road's blocked."

"Thank you," said Martha.

90

The corporal addressed Jerry. "What about you? These ladies with you?"

"Yes, sir," said Jerry. "We're trying to get to Reading, but we're lost."

"You sure are," said the corporal. "Is that you, the Chevvy with the New York plates?"

"Yes, sir."

The corporal shook his head. "Give up, You're lucky you're in a hotel."

"Why?" said Jerry.

"There's no way to get to Reading tonight. West of here—no roads passable. You can't even get to Allentown."

"But we gotta work tonight," said Jerry. "We're supposed to be in Reading by eleven."

"You couldn't make it by eleven tomorrow morning, and I'm telling you now, don't try it. I'm warning you. You can't even get to Flour Mill, that's three miles from here, west."

"Holy God, we have a Legion date," said Jerry.

"I can't help that," said the corporal. "To tell you the truth, I wish you'd all stay here, you included, Lady. And the truck. He might get through, but he got a chance of not. It's gonna get worse before it gets better. Don't you have a radio, Mr. Studebaker?"

91

"Well, *I* don't have one. I'm kind of against them. But Mrs. Fenstermacher has a little one in the kitchen she listens to."

"The last report I got, it snowed ten inches since early this afternoon, and it isn't supposed to let up till morning. You people don't know when you're lucky. I wish I could hole up here for the night." He pulled on his gauntlets. "Good night all." He buckled up his collar and went out.

"Well, that's too bad for you folks," said Ira. "But we have plenty of room for all, and plenty to eat, and the place is nice and warm."

No one said anything.

"Even a doctor, in case we have any sickness," said Ira.

"I got a pain in the bankroll," said Jerry. "Can he fix that?"

Part Two

listening to her tiny radio, specifically to the Original Amateur Hour. Appropriately enough, the artist performing at that moment was a young man who made music by knocking on kitchen utensils. He was playing—also appropriately enough—"The World Is Waiting for the Sunrise" in fox-trot time. He finished to loud and sustained applause by the studio audience, but Mrs. Fenstermacher and her visitors ignored the announcer's statement to the effect that New York listeners who wanted to vote for Tony Furillo, the scullery virtuoso, could do so by telephoning a certain Luxemburg number, or in Chicago, the Honour City (by which he meant only that Chicago was the city being honoured that evening; he did not mean that Chicago is *the* Honour City), listeners could call a certain Dearborn number. His statement was lost on Marie Fenstermacher because Marie was surprised and not immediately pleased by the invasion of her kitchen by a very strange lot of people: a handsome woman in beautifully cut riding habit, black boots, a wilted stock, and no hat; two young women with too much make-up on, dyed black hair in page-boy bobs, black satin dresses that were cut too low in the bust and fitted too tightly almost

96

everywhere; a young man who belonged in the
Midway at the Allentown Fair; Dr. Graeff, with a
silly grin on his face, and Ira Studebaker, trying
to smile but—Marie Fenstermacher knew—a bit
uneasy to be participating in the invasion.

It was up to Ira to explain things. He said these
good people had been told by the highway patrol
that they might have to stay at the hotel all night,
on account of the roads. He didn't think they'd
had enough to eat, only those sandwiches. The
horseback-riding woman interrupted to say she
had enjoyed *her* steak sandwich, but could eat
another, and wanted to help. In fact, she said,
speaking for the others as well, they all wanted
to help. The others nodded and otherwise gave
sign that the horseback-riding woman was
speaking the truth.

Marie Fenstermacher did not like people
invading her kitchen any more than she liked
people helping her with the preparation of food,
and she had serious doubts as to the help she was
likely to get from this lot; but it was plain to see
that they *wanted* to help and their hearts were in
the right place, so—to Ira's relief—she said all
right and reached for pencil and paper to write
down the various orders.

97

The horseback-riding woman said she was going to have another steak sandwich, done the same way as the other one.

The Allentown Fair young man said if there was steak, enough steak, he'd have one too. He said he didn't know how the lady had had hers before, but just as long as it was steak and rare, that was for him. French fries, if it wasn't too much trouble.

The older of the two dressed-alike girls said she would like a couple of lamb chops, if they had them. She asked if there was any other kind of potatoes besides French fries, because she was told to stay off fried stuff. She was informed that she could have any kind of potatoes she wanted. She thought a moment and decided on mashed. She would have mashed.

The younger girl was in total agreement with the older girl; she wanted just what the older girl ordered.

Mrs. Fenstermacher interrupted the giving and taking of orders to announce, for the benefit of Ira and Dr. Graeff, that she had a roast chicken in the oven, if they were interested. Dr. Graeff said all he wanted was a piece of pie and a cup of coffee, but Mrs. Fenstermacher told him that when he had a chance to eat some decent food,

to get each other's names straight and thought
she would start with herself by saying that she
was Mrs. Paul. She said, without making a big
thing of it, that the man with her, the man, that
is, who was outside working on the car, was not
her husband, but she could understand why people
made that mistake. Easy mistake to make. Then
she made sure she had Mrs. Fenstermacher's
name right, and introduced the Pickwicks and
Jerry to her. They were all polite even the Allentown Fair young man. And with the name business
all straightened out, the horseback lady, Mrs.
Paul, that is, took off her jacket, thus revealing
that she was wearing a sweater under the jacket
and a mannish shirt under the sweater. Apologising
for the wilted condition of the stock, she unpinned,
untied and unbuttoned it and took it off. She
asked Mrs. Fenstermacher where she could put
those things, and Mrs. Fenstermacher directed
her to a clothes closet in the short hallway between
the kitchen and the dining-room. Mrs. Paul, return-
ing, rolled up her sleeves and turned in her shirt
collar to make a neat and modest V at the throat.
She told Mrs. Fenstermacher she was ready to
go to work, and Mrs. Fenstermacher got her an
apron out of the bottom drawer. It made quite

a difference, the transformation from a young woman in riding breeches and man's shirt to a young woman in an apron with its smooth white line down her bosom. When she turned around, there were the breeches and boots, but in the front she looked very pleasing and feminine.

The Allentown Fair young man, Mr. Mayo, asked if there was an apron to fit him, and Mrs. Fenstermacher did not know whether to take him seriously or not but said if he really meant it he could wear the hired girl's apron, which was hanging on the pantry door. He said he really meant it, got the apron and put it on, and the Pickwick sisters burst into giggles, but stopped their laughter as quickly as it started, and offered to put on aprons themselves, if there were any. Mrs. Fenstermacher thought there might be one of hers and one of the hired girl's in the bottom drawer. She was right, and the girl named Paulette put on Mrs. Fenstermacher's extra apron and the girl named Conchita put on the hired girl's.

Ira came back from the garage and told Marie Fenstermacher that the lady's husband would have another steak sandwich, the same as before; that the truck driver hadn't wanted anything on first inquiry, but under persuasion agreed to eat a

101

cold roast-beef sandwich; and that Charles Mannering would share the roast chicken with Ira and Dr. Graeff.

That was easy, Mrs. Fenstermacher declared, and said she could do it herself unless Mrs. Paul really wanted to help. Mrs. Paul said she wasn't really doing Mrs. Fenstermacher a favour. She said she liked working around a kitchen. Paulette Pickwick said she did too, although she wasn't much good at it. Conchita Pickwick said she wasn't much good at it either, but could wash or dry the dishes. Paulette said she would wash if Conchita would dry, and Mrs. Paul said she was glad someone else had volunteered to do the dishes because that was the one thing she did not like to do, Mrs. Fenstermacher concurring.

Reading from her list Mrs. Fenstermacher rechecked the orders with Mrs. Paul. There were three steak sandwiches, cut thin and rare; one order French fries; two lamb chops—four lamb chops actually—and two mashed potatoes; three for roast chicken, and one cold roast beef. Mrs. Fenstermacher thought she would handle the steaks and French fries if Mrs. Paul would take care of the chops and mashed potatoes. The roast chicken was taken care of and was being kept warm

102

in the oven. The cold roast-beef sandwich presented no problem.

In a kind of aside Mrs. Fenstermacher remarked
that this was hardly any meal at all compared
with the meals she had prepared in the past and
hoped to prepare in the future. A real Pennsylvania Dutch supper, the kind they hoped to
specialize in to attract the public, would have
the meal begin with oysters on the half shell,
followed by thick chicken noodle soup, stewed
chicken, mashed potatoes, candied sweet potatoes,
string beans, lima beans, pickled beets, creamed
carrots, squash, endive salad, dozens of waffles,
apple pie, cream pie, shoofly pie, hot or cold
mince pie, rhubarb pie, coconut cake, chocolate
cake with vanilla icing and angel food with
chocolate icing. And besides, on the table would
be the seven sweet and seven sour relishes,
somersausage, bologna, liverwurst, and for after
dinner there would be peppermints, macaroons,
and spun-sugar kisses. And there would be a pitcher
of milk and a pitcher of beer on the table. Mrs.
Paul said she had read about that kind of meal
in a recent novel, but didn't see how it could be
possible, but Mrs. Fenstermacher assured her it
was true. Not only was it no exaggeration, but

103

there were plenty of good eaters who would ask for seconds and thirds on everything, she said. The meal they were about to prepare was hardly more than short-order cooking, she said. It presented no real problem. Dr. Graeff, listening to Mrs. Fenstermacher's description of a real Pennsylvania Dutch meal, not only corroborated it but added that it was such meals that kept the doctors in business. There ensued some slight discussion between the doctor and Mrs. Fenstermacher, with Mrs. Fenstermacher maintaining that good hearty eating never hurt anybody and that the longevity of Macungie County people as against the early mortality of city people proved her point. The doctor gently suggested her vital statistics were at fault, since it was his impression that city people lived longer than country people, and 1950 people lived longer than, say, 1890 people. Mrs. Fenstermacher said that was nonsense, and all you had to do was look around you in the city and in the country, and where would you see more old people? Rather pointedly she declared that people that didn't like to eat were not good-natured, and she told Mrs. Paul that half the time Dr. Graeff forgot to eat anything at all.

Mrs. Fenstermacher then got the meats from the cold-room, a built-in cell opening off the kitchen. The steaks, she said, would take twenty minutes; ten minutes on each side, and while she was doing the steaks the French fries would be cooking. Mrs. Paul could be mashing the potatoes while the chops were being broiled, and the chops would take about twenty minutes too. So would the coffee. They would get the coffee started when they put the steaks on. Mrs. Fenstermacher said she would slice the chicken unless Mrs. Paul wanted to do it, and Mrs. Paul thought Mrs. Fenstermacher would do a better job.

They went to work and the Pickwick sisters sat at the kitchen table, trying to take an interest, but obviously feeling rather out of things at this stage of the game. They were more than a little surprised to see that Mrs. Paul could be efficient with a potato masher; this, however, did not hold their attention for long. Their friend Mr. Mayo went down-cellar and brought up a couple of scuttles of coal for the range, and then he and Dr. Graeff, at the latter's suggestions, made themselves scarce, or went to the bar. The doctor was back a minute later, asking the women if he couldn't bring them all a little liquid refresh-

105

ment. After some demurring the Pickwicks said they would have an Old Fashioned with everything in it, and Mrs. Paul said she would wait a while.

They heard the men come in from the garage and then Howard Pomfret entered the kitchen. He stopped when he saw Martha in her apron in front of the range, then he went over and kissed her cheek. She smiled at him and patted his own cheek and introduced him to Mrs. Fenstermacher, who could not hide the fact that she was shocked by this demonstration of affection by two people who were not married. Mrs. Paul, for the benefit of Mrs. Fenstermacher as well as for Howard Pomfret's benefit, repeated her earlier remark that they were not married, but were going to be. She also told Howard Pomfret that everybody had *thought* they were married but she didn't see any use in deceiving people. He made no comment on the wisdom of her decision, since it was not the time or the place for such comment. He told her that the trouble had not been in the distributor or the starter but in the gas line. He said the truck driver fellow, Joe Rogg by name, spotted the trouble right away and had just finished correcting it. He said he was going to buy Rogg

106

a drink, and Martha Paul asked him to keep
Rogg's drinks to an absolute minimum, that he
had had quite a few and had been warned by the
policeman not to have any more. Howard Pomfret
said that Rogg had refused to take any money
for his services. He said Rogg had seemed quite
surprised at being invited to have supper with
the crowd; had there been any trouble? Martha
said there had not been any trouble, not really.

Howard Pomfret left the women and joined the
men in the bar.

Charles was at his post behind the bar, having
neatened up after his efforts to start the station
wagon.

Ira, standing at the customer's side of the bar,
was gripping a bourbon and soda but not drinking it.

Dr. Graeff was conversing with Jerry Mayo.

Joe Rogg, the truck driver, was in the men's
room.

Howard Pomfret told Charles he would have a
Scotch and water. He took a position to the left
of Ira and to the right of Dr. Graeff. The doctor
made room for him but continued his conversation
with Jerry.

Jerry: "You may be right, Doc, but I'm gonna
keep my distance."

Dr. Graeff: "Keep your distance, sure, but don't get sarcastic with him. Don't make a fool of him. Big fellows like him, they aren't apt to be quick-witted, so when you get sarcastic with him the only thing he can think of is hitting you. Handle him right and he won't be any trouble."

Jerry: "I don't want any trouble. I just wish he'd get the hell outa here. I'm a lover of peace."

Dr. Graeff: "Well, I guess we all are."

Jerry: "Not him when he keeps clouting himself over the head with that straight rye."

Dr. Graeff: "Well, just you don't get sarcastic with him and he'll soon be gone. He only ordered a cold roast-beef sandwich, so I don't think he's planning to be here long."

Jerry: "Here he is . . . And like I told you, uh, we came through the Holland Tunnel and got as far as Easton, P A, without any trouble, but then . . ."

Joe Rogg, rubbing his hands, joined Ira and Howard Pomfret. He was in a pleasant mood and it was plain to see that he liked Pomfret, the affinity between large men. Rogg was the taller by an inch or so, but Pomfret was so much taller than Ira, Dr. Graeff and Jerry that he and the truck driver were the big men in the room. (Charles, being behind the bar and being slender, did not count.) Joe Rogg gave Pomfret a friendly thump on the arm and put a hand on Ira's shoulder.

"This is my pal," said Joe, "this big son of a bitch."

Pomfret smiled. "Your pal wants to buy you a drink."

"No, no," said Joe Rogg. "I'll buy you a drink. Buy everybody a drink. Hey, Doc. Hey, you, Doc."

"Yeah?" said Dr. Graeff.

"How much do I owe from before? I had a couple before," he explained to Ira and Charles. "The doc was bartending. How much was it?"

"Oh, I think it was three ryes," said the doctor.

"Three? Only three?" said Joe Rogg. "I had three, but didn't I buy you one?"

"Well, maybe you did," said the doctor. "But I must have bought you one too. I think you owe for three."

"I got plenty of money," said Joe Rogg. "You don't believe that do you, you big son of a bitch?"

"Sure I believe it," said Pomfret.

"I got plenty," said Joe Rogg. "Take a look at this." He unbuttoned his shirt pocket and produced a quantity of paper money, folded lengthwise and then bent in the middle. "Ten, twenty, thirty, forty, fifty, sixty, seventy, eighty, ninety, *one* hundred, a hundred and twenty, hundred and forty, hundred and sixty, hundred and eighty, *two* hundred. Two-fifty, three hundred. Three-fifty, four hundred. Four-fifty, five hundred. Five-fifty, six hundred. Seven hundred. Eight hundred. Eight hundred bucks, brother. Don't you worry if I can't pay for the drinks."

"That's quite a bundle," said Mayo.

Joe Rogg looked at him. "You're God-damn right it is, little fellow."

"That's a lot of cash to carry around," said Ira.

"That's what I was thinking," said Pomfret.

"Somebody take it off me, you mean?" said Joe Rogg.

"Well, as Mayo said, it's quite a bundle, and if somebody saw you with it they might want to *try*, anyway," said Pomfret. "In fact, I'm tempted myself."

"Ah, you old son of a bitch, you're too honest. I can tell by lookin' at you," said Joe Rogg.

"Well, thanks. That isn't an opinion generally shared, but I'm glad you think I have an honest face," said Pomfret.

"You wouldn't have to stick me up or like that. Here, you want a hundred? Here," he held out a bill for Pomfret.

"Be careful, I might take you up on that," said Pomfret.

"What's a hundred dollars to you?" said Joe Rogg. "I can tell a millionaire when I see one. And not only the horseback-riding outfit. I knew a guy in the Army and all of us wearing fatigues, but I could tell him for a millionaire. I knew he was a millionaire just by looking at him." He put his hand on Ira's shoulder again. "This fellow, he got a little, but no millionaire. The doc, Christ, he ain't any millionaire. The little fellow there, he ain't got a pot to piss in. Am I right?"

"As far as I'm concerned," said Dr. Graeff.

"I know I'm not," said Ira.

"Not a pot," said Mayo.

"What about you, you old son of a bitch?"

"Well, right and wrong. My father had a million, or close to it. *I* never had," said Pomfret.

"Well, it's the same thing," said Joe Rogg.

"I wish I thought so," said Pomfret.

"Wud you do? I bet you blew it all on dames and booze, huh?" said Joe Rogg. "Your old man left it to you and you got rid of it."

111

"I distributed a fair sum, but nothing like a million," said Pomfret.

"Maybe Charlie there, maybe Charlie's a millionaire," said Joe Rogg.

"All in gilt-edged securities," said Charles.

"You're all right, Charlie. And a pretty good mechanic, too," said Joe Rogg.

"Uh-huh," said Charlie. "But don't offer me none of those C-notes. Us millionaires, you know us. We take anything we can lay our hands on. That's how we got to be millionaires."

"Don't worry, I ain't offering C-notes to any-body that's liable to take them. I'm no God-damn fool."

"What if I'd crossed you? What if I'd taken it?" said Pomfret. "I could have crossed you, you know."

"Yeah, but I knew you wouldn't," said Joe Rogg. "I'm no God-damn fool." He put the money back in his pocket and buttoned the flap, giving it a final pat. "You guys wonder how a guy pushing a truck can go around with over eight hundred bucks in his pocket."

"Why, I thought you fellows earned that much in a week," said Pomfret.

"In a pig's ass you did, you old son of a bitch,"

112

said Joe Rogg. "We do all right, don't worry about us——"

"I can vouch for *that*," said Ira.

"No, the way I got this dough," said Joe Rogg. "I bet."

"The horses?" said Pomfret.

"The hell with the horses. That's for suckers. Nobody ever beat the horses. I bet on football games. I got twenty or thirty bets going every Saturday. The garage where I work out of, and one over in Jersey where we all stop for coffee, guys that push the trucks. Wouldn't they rather bet with me, instead of some son of a bitch they don't know."

"Oh, you make book," said Mayo.

"I make bets. I don't make no God-damn book. I bet with guys that I know and they know me."

"But how do you know what prices to offer?" said Pomfret.

"Oh, I get a sheet and I offer the same prices as the sheet," said Joe Rogg.

"Isn't that dangerous?" said Pomfret.

"Who to? You mean I'm muscling in?" Joe Rogg grinned. "Sure I am, I'm muscling in. But they didn't say anything so far. When they say anything maybe I'll handle it one way and maybe

113

I'll handle it the other. Maybe they'll want me to join up with them, but maybe I won't wanta do that. Maybe I'll just turn him over my knee and give him a spanking, the guy that talks to me."

"I always thought they were tougher than that," said Pomfret.

"Well, I'm pretty tough, too," said Joe Rogg. "And maybe they'll want me with them."

"Is Harvard going to win this week?" said Pomfret.

"It's not who wins. It's points," said Joe Rogg.

"I know," said Pomfret. "I was just wondering."

"They never win, Harvard. But you can win on points."

"Gentlemen—" it was Martha. "Dinner is served."

Joe Rogg swallowed his drink. He put his arm around Pomfret's shoulder. "You son of a bitch, you can pick them all right."

Now the men trooped out of the bar, across the lobby and into the dining-room—all the men save one, Howard Pomfret. He lingered as they were leaving the bar, long enough to be the last, but not so far behind the others that he was

114

separated by any large distance. The dining-room door was wide open, and Martha in her apron was standing on the lobby side of the dining-room, with her hand outstretched in a gesture of invitation, a little like a tea-room hostess.

Howard Pomfret, seemingly in the file of men and playing the game of tea-room customer, got just to within touching range of Martha and then, about to pass her, he snatched the outstretched hand and pulled her from the doorway. He held her to him and kissed her.

"I never loved anybody this way," he said.

"Am I your final love?" she said. "You said I was."

"My final love," he said.

"We'll tell Alex tonight, when we get home," she said.

"Why do you want to tell him tonight?" he said.

"So I can stay with you tomorrow night," she said.

"You can stay with me tonight, here," he said. "These people don't care. They expect us to."

"Maybe they do, but it'll spoil it for them," she said.

"Spoil it for them? How?"

115

"It's something I have to tell you later, not now," she said. "Now let's go in, and you be nice to everybody, because I'm happy."

"I love everybody," he said. "Everybody."

She smoothed his hair and wiped the lipstick off his mouth and they went in together. The others, all but Mrs. Fenstermacher, were standing, waiting for them, and grinning, not unlike people waiting outside the church to have a look at the bride.

"Well, where shall we sit, Mrs. Paul? Do you want to arrange us?" said Ira.

"Me? Well, all right," said Martha. She, with some assistance from the Pickwicks, had already set the table. "Let's see, is Charles going to sit with us? I think it'd be nice."

Charles, coming in from the kitchen, said: "No, ma'am, thanks, but I got my job to do, that's waiting on this table." He was firm and sincere, and Martha did not belabour the point. He was going to share the roast chicken with Ira and Dr. Graeff—two roast chickens, as it turned out— and he really wanted to eat alone.

"Well, let's see," said Martha. "The table has room for twelve, and without Charles we're nine. Nine means two men will have to sit side by side,

116

somewhere. We'll start at the head of the table. Mr. Studebaker. Then me, I'm going to put myself on your right. Mr. Mayo next to me. Howard, you and Mr. Mayo sit next to each other, and then Mrs. Fenstermacher at that end. On her right, Dr. Graeff. Next to you, Conchita Pickwick. Then Mister——"

"Joe Rogg's the name," said Joe Rogg.

"Mr. Rogg, I'll put you between the Pickwick sisters, and there we are. It's not perfect, but it's the best I can do," said Martha.

"*I* think it's perfect," said Ira.

"I think it works out fine," said Dr. Graeff.

"Charles, will you tell Mrs. Fenstermacher— any time?" said Martha.

"Yes, ma'am," said Charles.

Mrs. Fenstermacher came in from the kitchen and took the place reserved for her and they all sat down. There was a momentary lull until Martha, a trifle self-consciously, devoted herself to Ira Studebaker. "Well, I think this is very pleasant," she said. "I'm not only a guest at your first dinner, I even helped a little in preparing it."

"A little?" said Ira. "You did half, that's not a little. I'd say that was quite a lot for a guest.

117

Maybe I ought to offer you a job, but I guess you'd come pretty high."

The others listened carefully to every word, then Howard made the conversational effort with Mrs. Fenstermacher. "This is quite an old place, I imagine," he said. "I'm glad Mr. Studebaker kept the old things. I hate to see the old things go."

"He didn't only keep the old things," she said. "He went out and bought everything he could lay his hands on, old. He was around at auctions and sheriff's sales till we got more here than we got room for. Down-cellar we got piled up chairs and settees. Maybe we ought to have a sale ourselves." From there they progressed to some of the history of the hotel, thus bringing in Dr. Graeff and his recollections. Conchita Pickwick listened and nodded to every statement of fact.

Paulette Pickwick, not pretending that she had got the best of the seating bargain, made her own conversational effort. "Are you from this place?" she said.

"No. Where you from?" said Joe Rogg.

"New York," she said.

"New York City?" he said.

"That's right," she said.

118

"Is this kid your sister? She don't look like you,"
he said.

"We're supposed to look a lot alike."

"No," he said. "Why do you wear the same
kind of clothes?"

"Didn't you get the name? We're the Pickwick
Sisters," said Paulette. "We're in show business."

"On the stage? What do you do? What kind
of an act do you put on?"

"We sing and dance," said Paulette.

"Yeah? What does *he* do, the little fellow?"

Jerry Mayo, not usually a man to be left out
of a conversation, had been the silent one while
Martha was talking to Ira and Pomfret to Mrs.
Fenstermacher. Rather than remain silent he took
up Joe Rogg's question: "I'm a weight-lifter,"
he said.

"You a weight-lifter?" said Joe Rogg.

"Military press. Snatch and grab. Sure," said
Jerry.

"How much can you lift?"

"I was only kidding. I'm lucky if I can lift the
tab for the supper," he said.

"Well then what do you do?" said Joe Rogg.
He whispered to Paulette: "Is he your pimp?"

"Lay off, lay awf-f-f," said Paulette.

119

Martha, suspecting trouble when she saw Rogg whispering to Paulette, turned her attention to Jerry and the threatened situation did not develop.

The serving of the food, done expeditiously by Charles, gave them all something to watch and the food gave them something to do with their hands. Joe Rogg, of course, with his cold roast-beef sandwich, used his hands and nothing else. He finished his sandwich, before anyone else was half finished, and at Ira's urging he ordered another. Charles brought him the second sandwich and also announced that there was cider if anybody wanted it, and beer, if anybody wanted it. Nobody wanted cider; the Pickwicks and Mrs. Fenstermacher were the only ones who did not want beer.

Ira and Mrs. Fenstermacher helped Charles to take away the dishes and to serve the dessert. Martha, Jerry, Howard, Joe Rogg, Dr. Graeff and Ira had hot apple pie. The Pickwicks and Mrs. Fenstermacher had pumpkin pie and cider, Mrs. Fenstermacher having changed her mind and the minds of the Pickwicks.

Ira excused himself and went upstairs and came down with the humidor that had been given him on his retirement from the fruit and produce business. All the men took cigars and the women rose, as one, and cleared the table. While the women were working the men discussed weather conditions. Charles joined them. "I got the bum's rush out of the kitchen," he said. He sat at the table with the other men and had himself a cigar.

They had had enough to eat to make them comfortable without feeling sleepy. It was a satisfactory meal in every sense of the word. "Just right," said Jerry Mayo. "I don't even want another cup of coffee."

"I feel like getting out my old trombone," said Charles.

"Why don't you?" said Ira. "Charles is a real jack-of-all-trades. You ought to hear him play a musical instrument."

"There's a fellow in the band where I come from——" said Joe Rogg.

"Do you play slide or valve?" said Dr. Graeff. "I didn't know you could play the trombone. I took lessons myself, when I was a boy."

"Both," said Charles. "But I got rid of my valve some years back. I got rid of it trying to make eight the hard way. That was some years back."

121

"Say, I got a pair of dice here in my pocket," said Joe Rogg.

"Let's hear some music," said Howard Pomfret. "A good meal—my second—and a good cigar. I think it'd be nice to hear some music."

Joe Rogg tossed his dice on the table and leaned forward to see what he had thrown. "A big ten," he said. He stripped a twenty-dollar bill from his wad. "Any part of it. Two to one no ten?" He looked at Howard. "Come on, you old son of a bitch."

"Trombone's up in my room. I'll be right back," said Charles.

"No, if we start shooting crap we'll be here all night," said Howard.

"Who says we're *not* gonna be here all night?" said Jerry.

"*We're* not," said Howard. "We have to get moving very soon."

"Who don't? I gotta start pushing that milk," said Joe Rogg.

"Let's not have any gambling," said Ira. "I like a friendly game of poker and all, but not in here. It wouldn't look right if somebody came in."

"I agree with Ira," said Dr. Graeff.

122

"Anyway, I might get lucky and take away your eight hundred dollars," said Howard.

"Well, put up some money and maybe you will," said Joe Rogg. "Come on, you old son of a bitch."

"No thanks," said Howard.

Charles, bearing the trombone in its case, was back quickly and a little out of breath. He placed the case on the table, nudging the dice toward Joe Rogg. He removed the trombone and played a couple of fast scales.

"Knows how, all right," said Jerry.

"Any request numbers?" said Charles.

" 'Getting Sentimental Over You'." said Jerry.

Charles smiled at him. "I know what you're thinking," he said. "Try him on a hard one. Okay."

He played a chorus of the song, duplicating every note, if not quite the tone, of the Tommy Dorsey recording, faltering only slightly on the two higher notes in the middle part. He was playing the last four bars when the kitchen door opened and Conchita, tea-towel in hand, stood and listened.

"Play it again," she said. She did not have to say please. Please was in the way she said it.

Charles nodded and played it again, better.

He finished and she nodded and went back to the kitchen.

"Is that her favourite?" said Howard.

"You got *me*," replied Jerry, then: "Yes."

"Play 'Tiger Rag'," said Joe Rogg.

"Oh, God no," said Jerry.

"He played what *you* wanted," said Joe Rogg.

"I'll play it," said Charles. "I'll play anything I know." Joe Rogg shouted "Hold that tiger!" all through the playing. In the second chorus, which he requested, he also kept time with himself, although not with Charles, by beating on the table.

"Mr. Pomfret?" said Charles.

"I'll think of something," said Pomfret.

"Charles, do you know one I'd like to hear?" said Ira.

"What's that, Mr. Studebaker?" said Charles.

"Well, it's a hymn. 'Nearer My God to Thee'," said Ira.

"Jesus Christ!" said Joe Rogg.

"That's the general idea," said Jerry, *sotto voce* to Howard Pomfret.

"Stop needling him. He's apt to take a poke at you," said Pomfret.

Charles commenced to play the hymn and was

124

joined by Joe Rogg singing: "Nero my dog has fleas," every time the theme was repeated.

The hymn was finished and Charles asked Dr. Graeff for his selection. "I liked *that*," said the doctor. "But I have one, I don't know if you know it. It's a college song. 'Far Above Cayuga's Waters'."

"Sure I know it," said Charles.

"Did you go to Cornell, Doctor?" said Howard.

"I went to Penn, but I always liked that song." said Dr. Graeff.

The women began coming in during the Cornell song, and by the time Charles had finished they had taken the places they occupied at supper.

"How about 'Fair Harvard'?" said Pomfret.

"I don't think I know that one," said Charles. "Give me the first four bars, maybe I'll remember it."

Howard gave him the first three notes and Charles nodded. "I remember," he said. "But I have to play it in a different key." He played it and Howard sang it and Martha made a duet towards the end.

"I knew it by another name," said Charles. "The ladies have any preference? Mrs. Fenstermacher?"

"Oh, I don't know," she said. "Can you play 'Smiles'?"

Martha and Jerry were the only ones who knew the lyric, and they harmonized the last part.

"How did *you* know that?" asked Jerry.

"How did *you?* I'm older than you are," said Martha.

"How did *you*, Mrs. Paul? I used to sing it in the first War, but I didn't remember the words," said Dr. Graeff.

"Oh, I just know a lot of old songs," said Martha.

"She knows the words to every song that was ever written," said Howard Pomfret.

"Not *quite*," said Martha.

"You can't stump her," said Howard.

Paulette spoke up: "Uh, can you play 'A Pretty Girl Is like a Melody'?"

"Yes, ma'am," said Charles. "If you give me just a second, the *embouchure* is a little out of practice."

"I have an idea," said Martha. "Maybe the Pickwick Sisters would give us a song. Don't you sing together?"

"Yes," said Paulette.

126

"They sing together *when* they sing together," said Jerry Mayo.

"Get *him*," said Paulette, to no one.

"I'd love to hear you and I think so would everybody else," said Martha.

"Sing! Go ahead and sing!" said Joe Rogg.

"Well, all right," said Paulette. "I wish we had a piano."

"Maybe I got one in the car," said Jerry. "I'll go out and look."

"You don't have to crack wise," said Paulette.

"No," said Conchita.

"We have a piano," said Mrs. Fenstermacher. "What do you think that is over there?"

"Oh, I didn't see it," said Paulette.

"Paulette's a girl that lost two bass drums," said Jerry. "In one evening, yet."

"I did not, either," said Paulette.

"No," said Conchita.

"Oh, come on," said Martha. "You stop kidding and let them sing."

The willing hands of Ira Studebaker and Dr. Graeff lifted the black cotton cover off the piano, and Joe Rogg and Howard Pomfret pushed it closer to the table. Jerry dragged a chair to the piano and sat down and the Pickwicks, taking off their aprons and slicking down their dresses, assumed their positions beside Jerry. They were immediately professional, with the smiles and every slight gesture calculated and rehearsed. They were in another world (their own), and instead of an audience of seven they might have been performing before seven hundred. The Pickwicks stood with arms linked, looking down at Jerry. Jerry looked up at them, then at the audience, then at the girls.

"A little song, a little song entitled—'Father Left His Choon Gum on the Bedpost Overnight'."

Paulette broke away from Conchita—part of the act—and faced her audience. She held her hands clasped in a prayerful attitude and closed her eyes and began to vocalize like an opera star. "La dee-ee-ee da, da dee da."

Jerry struck some discords in the bass. "A little song, a little song entitled—'Father Cut Your Toenails, You're Tearing All the Sheets'."

It was Conchita's turn to play classical, and she sang a scale, but on the final note she did a bump and immediately Jerry began to play, and the Pickwicks began to sing, in fast time: "Mississippi Mud". Jerry joined in the singing doing the Crosby part, while Paulette did the Rinker part

128

and Conchita the Barris part. They finished together, the girls bowed together, showing an abundance of bosom, and the audience applauded. Even Mrs. Fenstermacher, who had sat up straight suddenly at Conchita's bump, clapped her hands and laughed. Joe Rogg did not laugh, but he applauded and did not take his eyes off Conchita. The number was a genuine success, rhythmic, fast, sock; Paulette had shed the five years' difference between herself and Conchita, and Conchita, with her youth and superb body—the legs were a trifle chunky—was cute and appealing.

Martha whispered to Howard: "Atlantic City?"

"She's not bad," he said.

Jerry addressed the audience: "Do you want the works? The act runs a little over twenty minutes. The Pickwicks have a coupla dance routines. . . ."

"Let's have the works," said Howard.

"The works!" said Joe Rogg.

"Everything," said Mrs. Fenstermacher.

Charles, Dr. Graeff, and Ira applauded.

"The girls'll have to change their shoes, so I'll fill in with a little piano. Maybe Charles could be talked into a small session. Wuddia say, Charles?" Jerry clapped his hands in authentic master-of-ceremonies fashion and the others clapped their

129

hands in authentic audience-led-by-master-of-ceremonies fashion.

"I don't have to be persuaded," said Charles.

While the girls were changing to their tap shoes Charles and Jerry played "Rose Room" and "I Cover the Waterfront", and after that the Pickwick Sisters & Mayo—the name of the act—did the works and two encores.

"Before I tear myself away from the piano," said Jerry. "I got a sneaking suspicion Mrs. Paul makes with the voice. Wuddia say, Mrs. Paul?"

With only a little urging Martha got up, and accompanied for the first chorus by Jerry and for the second chorus by Jerry and Charles, she sang: "I Only Have Eyes for You". Her voice was an unprofessional mezzo-soprano; it was not Swarthout, but it was true and she had her own charm. She would not give an encore, but returned to her chair—formerly Jerry's chair—beside Howard Pomfret.

"Well, let's see," said Jerry. "How about some more hidden talent? The doctor. Doc, you said you used to play slide trombone. How about it?"

"No, no, no, no, no," said the doctor. "I'll be glad to sing a duet with Mr. Pomfret, if he wouldn't mind——"

130

"Maybe he has some other hidden talent," said Jerry. "Maybe he'd like to sing a solo."

"Not me," said Pomfret. "I'll take my chances with the doctor. What shall we sing, Doctor?"

They went into a huddle—the doctor, Pomfret, and Jerry, and after rejecting several of each other's suggestions they agreed upon a song: "By the Old Mill Stream". Pomfret took the tenor part, the doctor the melody. They had to make a second start because the doctor got carried away with the tenor part and forgot that he was to sing the melody. On the second attempt they did rather nicely. Following the precedent established by Martha they gave no encore.

"All right," said Jerry. "Quit while you're ahead. How about our friend the milkman? Got any songs or dances or witty sayings?"

"Who, me?" said Joe Rogg. "Not me. I can do a trick though. You want to see it?"

"A card trick?" said Jerry.

"No, another kind of a trick," said Joe Rogg. "I can do a couple. Get me a bottle of beer, and don't open it."

Charles brought a bottle of beer from the bar and handed it to Joe Rogg. He then bit the cap off. "Can anybody else do that?"

If anybody else could there were no volunteers.

"Show you another trick," said Joe Rogg. He placed a chair to his right, an ordinary bentwood chair. He grasped the bottom of the left rear leg, stiffened his arm and lifted it shoulder high. "It looks easy, but it ain't. Anybody want to try it?"

"I bet I could do it," said Conchita.

"What'll you bet? A kiss?" said Joe Rogg.

"I'll bet fifty cents," said Conchita.

"I don't want fifty cents, I got plenty of money. Come on, bet the kiss."

"All right," said Conchita. She tried to lift the chair but it fell out of her hand. "You win."

"I'll collect later," he said.

"Collect now," said Conchita.

"Not me, not in front of everybody," said Joe Rogg. "I'll collect any time I want to. You didn't say nothin' when I was to collect it."

"But neither did you," said Martha. "She's ready to pay off. She didn't bet a necking party."

"Did anybody ask for your advice? I didn't hear nobody asking for your advice," said Joe Rogg.

"I know," said Martha. "I volunteered it.

132

Conchita, give the man his kiss and that will be that."

Conchita, frightened and showing it, went up to Joe Rogg and attempted to kiss him without otherwise touching him, but when she got that close he grabbed her and held her with one hand about her waist. He squeezed her breast and put his hand between her legs and felt her behind. She struggled free and he let her go, laughing, as Pomfret reached them and gave the truck driver's shoulder a hard shove. Still laughing Rogg threw a punch at Pomfret but missed completely. "Do you wanta fight?" said Joe Rogg.

"Just leave her alone," said Pomfret.

"He's been a God-damn nuisance all evening," said Jerry Mayo.

"He has indeed," said Martha.

"I knew there'd be trouble," said the doctor.

"Well, then I guess it's time for you to go," said Pomfret to Joe Rogg.

"Who's gonna make me? You? You and who else?" said Joe Rogg.

"Me, maybe," said Charles.

"*You*, for Christ's sake?" said Joe Rogg.

"Well, me and this," said Charles. He put out

133

his hand, in it lay a .38 automatic. "It ain't no water pistol."

Joe Rogg looked at the pistol and at Charles. For a matter of seconds, five or six long seconds, during which a man can run half of a hundred yards, no one moved. They all stared at Joe Rogg and he studied Charles. Then he made his decision. "You can all go —— yourselves," he said, and went out. He went to the lobby and picked up his cap and jacket, and they heard the door slam, then they heard the truck starting and moving away.

"Good riddance," said Paulette. She put her arm around Conchita. The women, especially Mrs. Fenstermacher, were indignant but at the same time embarrassed; indignant at the act of the passes Joe Rogg had made, and embarrassed to have been witnesses to it.

"Good riddance to bad rubbage," said Conchita.

"Yeah, we can get along without *that* one," said Jerry Mayo, and played a few chords, good chords they were, but they did not get anywhere; he could not think of a tune to play, and there were no requests. The party mood was wrecked, not to be restored. They were all glad Joe Rogg had departed; most of them secretly had been wishing he would not stay in the first place. But he had stayed and for a little while had been part of the party, and his leaving and the manner of his leaving brought an end to this party. There would conceivably be other parties, conceivably with the same people, but this party was over, and everyone knew it.

"It's too bad," said Howard Pomfret. "The poor slob did help with the station wagon. Can't take that away from him."

"He had to be good for something," said Charles.

"My thought exactly, Charles," said Dr. Graeff. "But he was a big bully."

"He doesn't know any better," was Ira's judgement.

"Well," said Martha. "We've got to get started."

"I wish you could stay," said Ira.

"Well, *you* know," said Martha.

"Yes, I guess so," said Ira. "Don't you want me to call up the highway patrol and check the roads again?"

"Yes, I think that'd be a good idea," said Howard Pomfret. He accompanied Ira to the lobby.

Martha turned to Jerry Mayo, beginning the round of farewells. "Thank you very much for everything," she said. "I suppose you'll be

135

spending the night and then back to New York."

"We don't have any choice in the matter now," said Jerry. "We're too late for Reading even if the snow all melted."

"Well, one consolation, I don't imagine the show went on during this storm. They very likely cancelled it, don't you think?" said Martha.

"I never thought of that," said Jerry. "I pictured them waiting up all night for the Pickwick sisters and Mayo. Maybe none of them showed. You give me an idea. I'll give them a bell and find out. Maybe they postponed it and we still got a job tomorrow night."

The others sensing that this was at least a semi-private conversation, made talk among themselves.

"I hope so," said Martha. "And I hope we'll run into your act somewhere some time."

"Lady, you'll never run into this act," said Jerry.

"Why not? I might. I go to night clubs, every time I go to New York," said Martha.

"You only saw part of the act," said Jerry. "The rest is strictly for stag smokers."

"Oh," said Martha.

136

"What you saw we put on when we think the cops are in the house."

"Oh, a strip tease?" said Martha. "Is that the rest of the act?"

"That's *most* of the act," said Jerry. "You don't think a Legion smoker would send all the way to New York for those lousy songs and dances."

"I thought they were pretty good," said Martha.

"A dime a dozen. When you're not any better than that you gotta take your clothes off, and that's what the Pickwicks do."

"What do you do, or had I better not ask?" said Martha.

"I'm the professor. I play the piano," said Jerry.

Martha smiled. "Well, if I were you I wouldn't say anything to Mrs. Fenstermacher," she said. "Tell me, I'm curious. It's none of my business, but is one of them your girl?"

"Paulette and I've been shacked up for five years."

"You're married to Paulette?" said Martha.

"No, just shacked up. She isn't divorced and I guess it's a good thing she isn't."

"Why?"

137

"Guess," said Jerry.

"You mean Conchita?" said Martha.

"We're stuck on one another, but she won't go for the kip because Paulette's a friend of hers."

"They're not sisters?"

"Hell, I introduced them."

"So you're in love with Conchita, but living with Paulette. It must be awkward."

"*Awkward!* Well, it won't be much longer."

"Then what'll happen to Paulette?"

"Look at it another way, Mrs. Paul. What's happening to Conchita? We want to get married and have a coupla kids."

"I suppose I was taking a very conventional attitude. *Me!*" said Martha.

"You're all right."

"Thank you. So are you," said Martha.

"Thanks. Well, here's *your* boy friend."

Howard already was in his polo coat. "The highway patrol said it'd be all right to take a chance, if we go by way of Dieglerville."

"Dieglersville," said Ira.

"So I think we'd better be on our way."

They said individual but brief good-byes. Ira went out to the station wagon with Martha and

Howard Pomfret. "Be careful," said Ira. "And remember you're always welcome here."

"We'll be back a year from today," said Howard.

"That's a promise," said Martha.

"And there won't be any trouble about registering," said Howard.

"I wouldn't of cared about that," said Ira. "But I'll be glad to see you Mr.-and-Mrs."

The snow was still falling but less heavily as the station wagon pulled away, headed for Dieglersville.

Jerry Mayo was standing at the lobby desk. "I registered for the three of us," he said.

Ira read the registry: Miss Paulette Pickwick, N. Y. City; Miss Conchita Pickwick, N. Y. City; Jerry Mayo, N. Y. City. "A double for the girls, a single for me," said Jerry.

Ira frowned. "Is that the way you *want* it to be? This is a respectable hotel, but the old saying, What I don't know won't hurt me."

"It's not the way I want it to be but it's the way it's going to be," said Jerry. "It'd take too long to explain."

"Maybe not as long as you think, Jerry," said Ira. "I have eyes."

"Pop, you're all right," said Jerry Mayo, clutching Ira's arm. "By the way, do we get professional rates?"

Ira laughed. "Why, yes, I guess so. You're professional people."

"Now another favour. Will you go in and break the news? You just say, 'Ladies, you're all registered. You two have Room 123, and Mr. Mayo is 321.' Can you handle that?"

"I guess," said Ira. "Anyway I'll try."

"I'll make a fast dive for the boys' room till you get them tucked in."

"They'll want to say good night to you," said Ira.

"Not tonight they won't," said Jerry Mayo.

"The best one to handle this is Charles," said Ira.

"Let Charles handle it. Just so I don't have to be alone with them before they hit the sack."

Ira shook his head. "I sure hope being a hotel-keeper is always going to be as interesting as this."

Part Three

NOW IT WAS past midnight and Ira Studebaker made a tour of the bar and the
lobby, like the tour described in the beginning of this narrative, with the difference that
this time he was putting things away that
needed putting away, and he was not expecting
or hoping for any visitors. He locked up the bottled
goods, keeping out one bottle in case he or Charles
felt like having a night-cap, and pocketed the
key. He left for Charles the task of disconnecting
the beer pump, but he washed and put away
the remaining unwashed glasses. He performed
little chores that needed no special skill, such
as smoothing out the tablecloths and empty-
ing ashtrays; the beer pump, for example, was
something he would not tamper with until
Charles had explained it thoroughly, and he
wrote a memorandum to himself: "Ask Chas.
explain pump, coils, etc." Ira, of course, knew
more than a little about refrigeration as a result
of his years in fruit and produce, but he was not
a man who believed in learning by making

mistakes if the mistakes were avoidable.

Ira switched off all the bar-room lights except one he had chosen as a night light, which hung over the cash register on the back bar. He smiled at the cash register; there was nothing in it. He stood a moment holding the swinging door and had a parting look at the bar-room furniture and fixtures. "I never would of thought," he said, then he let the door swing behind him and seated himself in the Morris chair near the lobby stove.

He examined a couple of his souvenirs: the dollar bill Charles had spent; the cheque from Howard Pomfret. He took out his wallet and put the souvenirs in it, and before putting it back in his pocket he studied the snapshot of Irma Studebaker in the isinglass window. He replaced the wallet in his hip pocket and now he noticed that he had left the humidor on the lobby desk. He got himself a cigar and lit it, tossing the match in the stove. Charles came in as he was shutting the stove door.

"Charles, I was just wondering about something. That match made me wonder. I redded up the bar, but I left those kitchen matches on the tables. Do you think that's safe?"

144

"Well, I tell you," said Charles. "I don't know how long it's gonna take the rats to find out we're back in business, but wherever you got any large quantity of food you're gonna have rats *trying* to get at it. And I heard of many's a fire being started by rats gnawing on matches. I recommend we don't leave matches around."

"I think you're right, and tomorrow I want you to show me how the bar pump works. Not tonight. I left it for you to take care of tonight, but tomorrow you explain the whole thing to me."

"I will. I'll take care of both matters now," said Charles.

He was gone a few minutes and when he returned Ira said: "I'm enjoying a last cigar. Would you care to have one?"

"Yes, I think I would," said Charles. "Over there in the humidor?"

"Yes, and I kept out a bottle of whisky, in case either of us felt like a night-cap."

"I put it away again," said Charles. "Do you want a night-cap?"

"To tell you the truth, not unless you do," said Ira.

"No thanks, I'll sleep sound without it," said Charles, lighting his cigar.

145

"Mrs. Fenstermacher go out the back way? She wasn't in to say good night."

"No, she's staying right here in the hotel. She went up with the young ladies, the Miss Pickwicks, and she's sleeping in the next room to theirs."

"Oh, I *see*," said Ira.

"Uh-huh, that's it," said Charles.

"She didn't have any nightgown, though. Or any of those things."

"Well, I guess Mrs. Fenstermacher can always manage. She does keep some things here. She took her brush and comb, and I guess she don't need any toothbrush, just a glass to rest them in for the night."

"Have a chair," said Ira.

"I'll take the rocker," said Charles.

The men sat quietly for a little while.

"A cigar goes good with a rocker," said Charles.

"Or a Morris chair," said Ira.

"I don't see how a man can get any pleasure out of a cigar unless he's sitting down relaxed. You take a man like that trouble-maker we had here this evening. I bet he drives along fifty-seventy miles an hour with a cigar in his mouth. He's sitting, but not relaxed."

146

"By the way, Charles," said Ira. "I didn't know you had a revolver."

"Oh, yes. Yes, I owned that revolver over fifteen years. It's a pistol, you know. You know the difference."

"I meant pistol."

"I have a per*mit* for it. New York State. I guess it *is* expired, but I did have one. That was when I was a special. Special policeman. I guess to tell you the truth I never did have a per*mit* for the pistol, but I had one for a revolver. That was when I was a payroll guard. After the first War I used to be a payroll guard for a small private bank in Harlem, New York City. I used to go along accompanying the payroll. They tell me it's harder to get a per*mit* now, but it wasn't then."

"A payroll guard, eh? That must have been interesting work," said Ira.

"It wasn't exactly payroll, like paying off employees of a company," said Charles. "To tell you the truth, Mr. Studebaker, it wasn't a regular bank either. It was some gamblers. But they got me my per*mit*. My wife got me out of that when she found out what it was. I told her it was payroll-guarding, but she found out."

147

"They find out everything," said Ira.

"They find out too much for their own good. That's why I'm a divorced man," said Charles. "Well, looks like we're off to a pretty good start, Mr. Studebaker. I don't guess there's much in the till, but anyway we're open."

"It'll take a little time. We can't expect too much all at once," said Ira. "I'd just as soon build gradually."

"That way you'll find out what to buy. Buying is how you go broke in this business, if you don't know how to order. By the end of this Winter we'll know how to do the winter-time ordering, then next Spring and Summer. A year from now you ought to start making a little money, and by then Mrs. Fenstermacher and I, we'll have some trained help. I mean local girls for waitresses. The one she got helping her now. I don't expect she'll work out very well, not in the dining-room. In the kitchen, maybe, but not in the dining-room."

"Well, she's only temporary," said Ira.

"I gather she's some relation to Mrs. Fenstermacher," said Charles.

"On her husband's side. A niece," said Ira.

"That's good," said Charles.

148

"Why?"

"Well, I just didn't think she was on *Mrs. Fenstermacher's* side of the family, but you never can tell."

"There's something on your mind," said Ira. "Is it something I ought to know?"

"It's only a story," said Charles. "This girl, Mrs. Fenstermacher's helper, I was trying to recollect who she resembled that I ever saw, and finally it came to me."

"You know me, Charles. I never get tired of your stories," said Ira.

"This one's funny if it wasn't so sad," said Charles. "Some years back I used to hang around the police station near where I lived in South Philly. I knew all the policemen, white and coloured, and I used to play pinochle with them. Well, this one night I was there hanging around and they had this girl—she was white—under arrest. About around seventeen years of age she was. So she signed a paper, a kind of confession, and while they were waiting for her daddy to come to the station house they showed me this paper. I never read anything like it in all my whole life. I won't even tell you, it was so bad. I just tell you this much: it said how

149

she took on something like twenty young fellows one right after the other, under the bridge. Not for money, either. She didn't get a nickel out of it. Fact is, one fellow gave her a black eye after he was through with her. So the police sent for her father and he come to the station house and the sergeant, he said, 'Mr. So-and-so, this is a terrible thing to have to show to a father, but you gotta read it. Your girl's been bad again.' So the old man took the paper and he looked at it and shook his head, my-my-my, and he hand it back to the sergeant and the sergeant said they were going to have to send the girl to the Protectory and the daddy said he guess that was the proper thing to do. Then he went home. But anyway after he went out the sergeant looked at me and I was feeling sorry for the old man, and the sergeant said: 'Don't feel sorry, Charlie. The old man can't read.' "

"Did the father know the sergeant knew he couldn't read?"

"Yes, sir," said Charles. "The old man didn't know what was written down on that paper, but he knew it had to be bad."

"That *is* a sad story," said Ira.

"It really happened," said Charles.

"It's hard to believe we have people like that in the world," said Ira.

"Happens to people can read, too," said Charles.

"Oh, I know that all right," said Ira.

Charles stopped rocking and sat up in his chair. "More visitors? I think we're getting more visitors."

He and Ira stood up and the lobby door opened and the corporal from the highway patrol came in.

"Corporal," said Ira. "Back for a cup of coffee?"

"Not this time," said the corporal. "Well— maybe I will have a cup of coffee."

"I'll make some fresh," said Charles.

"No, don't bother then," said the corporal. "I won't have time. I came for some information. Mr. Studebaker, those two people, the man and woman in the riding uniforms? Do you know their names?"

"Why, yes, I know their names. What's the trouble?" said Ira.

The corporal pulled up a chair and sank wearily down. He undid the leather throat latch of his jacket and reached inside for his cigarettes. He tapped a cigarette until it bent almost double.

He said: "They're dead," and then he looked at Ira.

"Dead? *Dead?* You mean killed?" said Ira.

"Yeah, killed," said the corporal.

"How?" said Ira.

"They got run into by that milk truck, the one was outside here, I told him to stop obstructing the highway," said the corporal.

"Corporal," said Charles. "The milk truck left here before they did and he was headed the same way, towards Dieglersville."

"I don't understand it," said Ira.

"The milk truck left here, and the way I understood, it was only one-way traffic from here to Dieglersville," said Charles.

The corporal nodded vigorously. "We figured all that out. The milk truck left here and then he must of pulled over up by Hummel's farm. The tracks show he pulled over where you go into Hummel's farm. There he stopped."

Ira re-lit his dead cigar. "Then the people came along in the station wagon and he followed them and hit them."

"That's what happened," said the corporal.

"He hit them from behind," said Ira.

152

"He hit them from behind with the diesel. The woman went through the windshield, and the fellow broke his neck. He was still alive when my buddy and I got there, but she was a mess. She must of bounced back and then through the windshield."

"Was she killed instantly?" said Ira.

"I hope so, I hope so," said the corporal. "We got an ambulance from the Clinic. We couldn't wake Graeff up. Langendorf, from the Clinic, he pronounced him dead, the fellow. You didn't have to take another look at *her*."

"What about the man driving the truck?"

"I don't know," said the corporal. "Do you have a drink? Whisky or something like that? She was pretty."

"Unlock it, here's the key," said Ira to Charles.

"She was pretty," said the corporal. "But not now. Listen, I didn't tell you the whole thing, for Christ's sake. The station wagon caught fire, that's how we got notified. Somebody called from Hummel's and said there was a car on fire and we got it on the two-way."

"The two-way radio?" said Ira.

"So we went towards Hummel's and there was the station wagon and the diesel. You could

153

read a paper. My buddy got *him* out, I got her out. I should of left her in. Wuddia thing *this* is, *ketchup*?" The corporal accepted the large whisky from Charles. With the other hand he indicated red stains on his jacket. He drank the whisky, gagging a little but forcing it all down. Then he became again a peace officer. "You know their names. We can trace the station wagon through the plates, but give me their names and save us the bother. His name?"

"His name?" said Ira.

"*Yes. His* name," said the corporal.

Ira bowed his head. "Corporal, there's a situation here where . . ."

"Where what? All I want's their names. He didn't have any identification on him, and I don't have all night." He had his book out and a fountain pen in his hand.

"They weren't married," said Ira.

"All right," said the corporal.

"She has a husband and a young daughter," said Ira. The corporal waited, not patiently.

"I guess you couldn't let on this happened down Montgomery County, or anything like that," said Ira. "You'll have a lot of accidents tonight."

154

The corporal looked away and put down his notebook and took a drag on his cigarette, but picked up his notebook again. "You can't cover this up, Mr. Studebaker. They're dead. There's some things can be covered up, but not when a fatal accident enters into it. In addition, we got here a criminal offence. Leaving the scene of an accident. The driver of the diesel. If you don't want to give me their *names*, but I'll appreciate your co-operation."

Ira nodded. "Howard Pomfret. P, o, m, f, r, e, t. New York City. Her name is Mrs. Alexander Paul, Philadelphia. P, a, u, l. Outside of Philadelphia, but it'll be in the suburban phone book."

The corporal remembered something. "That's right," he said. "The name came over earlier tonight. Alexander Paul. Station wagon. I didn't connect it up with this. It was supposed to be a stolen car, but I never figured them for a stolen car."

"It has to be reported the way it was?" said Ira.

"No way out of it," said the corporal. "I'd like to help you out where it was some minor offence. This is too big."

155

"Corporal," said Charles. "What about the fellow driving the truck?"

"Somewhere around. I don't know if he was hurt or what, but he wasn't anywhere near when we got there. He can't go far," said the corporal.

"As Joe Louis said, he can run, but he can't hide," said Charles. "This fellow can hide, but he can't run."

"He can't run far," said the corporal. "We didn't go after him, he won't be hard to follow in the snow."

"What happens when you get him?" said Charles.

"We'll hold him," said the corporal.

Charles turned to Ira. "They'll hold him," he said.

"I should of put the collar on him early this evening," said the corporal. "I saw him with the booze."

"Oh, well," said Charles. "You'll hold him."

The corporal rose. "Well, thanks. I got what I came for."

"Can I bring your buddy a drink?" said Ira.

"He never touches it," said the corporal.

"Be glad to make some coffee," said Charles.

"Don't have the time, thanks," said the corporal. "Maybe we'll be back this way, if you want to make some, but I doubt it."

"Did they take them to the hospital?" said Ira.

"Schillinger's Undertaking Parlour. He's the coroner over in Dieglersville. Well, good night, men. Maybe see you later," said the corporal.

Ira and Charles accompanied him to the door.

They watched the car going away and returned to the rocker and the Morris chair.

"Mr. Studebaker, are you thinking the same thing I am?"

"It was deliberate?" said Ira.

"He waited for them," said Charles. "He banged into them on purpose."

"Maybe he didn't mean to kill them," said Ira.

"You think too much good of people," said Charles.

"I try," said Ira.

"The cop wished he would of arrested Mr. Joe Rogg. I wished I'd of shot him."

"I'm glad you didn't," said Ira.

"So am I, I guess, but I had the chance."

"It would have been cold blood. You couldn't do that."

"Maybe not," said Charles. "Well, he won't get away with it."

"Not if I can help it," said Ira.

"What can you do?"

"I don't know, but something," said Ira.

"He didn't like me, either," said Charles.

"His trouble, he didn't like anybody," said Ira. "Charles, you go to bed. You worked hard today."

"That? Work? I didn't hardly lift a finger to what I'm accustomed to."

"Go on, now. I know you're sleepy," said Ira.

"Well, you say the word sleepy and I get a bit drowsy," said Charles. He rose. "What about you, Mr. Studebaker?"

"I'll just stay here till the fire goes out," said Ira.

"You want me to bank it for you?" said Charles.

"No, thanks, I'll just wait till it goes out of its own accord," said Ira.

"You want the loan of my gun?" said Charles.

Ira smiled. "If he comes around this way I'll call you."

"Okay," said Charles. "Well, good night."

"Good night, Charles," said Ira.

Charles slid his hand up the banister and was gone.

For a long time Ira Studebaker gazed at the stove, and then the lobby got cold and he fell asleep.